The Pirate's Revenge

by L. N. Cronk

with

Heather Frey Blanton

Edited by Barbie Halaby

Published by Rivulet Publishing

Front Cover Photography (youth) by Micke Ovesson.

ISBN 978-0-9913812-1-0

Library of Congress Control Number: 2014912349

Scripture taken from the King James Version of the Bible (1611).

Spanish translations provided by Vicki Oliver Krueger.

Published by Rivulet Publishing
West Jefferson, NC, 28694, U.S.A.

Dedicated in memory of my father, S. Perry Nugent.

~L.N. Cronk

To Whit and Wyatt, and Capt. Carl, my beloved crew of scallywags!

~Heather Frey Blanton

For if that first covenant had been faultless, then should no place have been sought for the second. For finding fault with them, he saith, Behold, the days come, saith the Lord, when I will make a new covenant with the house of Israel and with the house of Judah: Not according to the covenant that I made with their fathers in the day when I took them by the hand to lead them out of the land of Egypt; because they continued not in my covenant, and I regarded them not, saith the Lord. For this is the covenant that I will make with the house of Israel after those days, saith the Lord; I will put my laws into their mind, and write them in their hearts: and I will be to them a God, and they shall be to me a people: And they shall not teach every man his neighbour, and every man his brother, saying, Know the Lord: for all shall know me, from the least to the greatest.
Hebrews 8:7-11

~ ~ ~

Table of Contents:

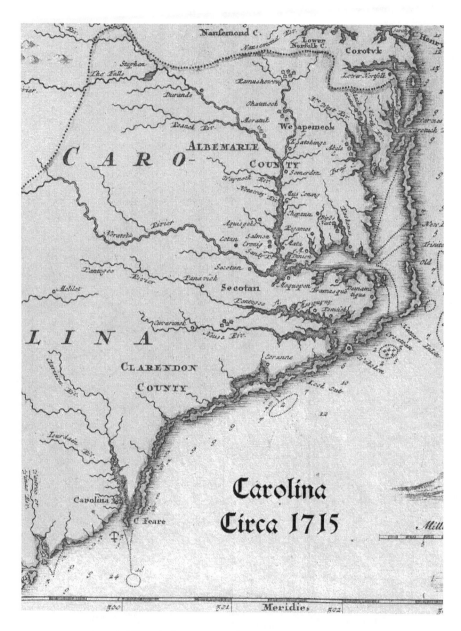

Adapted from J. B. Homann's c. 1715 map
of Virginia, Carolina, Maryland, and New Jersey.

Dearly beloved, avenge not yourselves, but rather give place unto wrath: for it is written, Vengeance is mine; I will repay, saith the Lord.

—Romans 12:19

~ ~ ~

Prologue
1717–1718

The wealthy plantation owner Stede Bonnet was well respected by the best of Bridgetown society. A retired British Army major, Bonnet was married with three children and—by all appearances—led an enviable life. To the shock and dismay of his family and friends, Bonnet suddenly abandoned his pampered life and left Barbados in a newly purchased ship, which he named the *Revenge*.

He did not even say goodbye to his wife.

Bonnet and his hired crew of approximately 70 men quickly became successful pirates. Within a year and a half, Bonnet captured many ships, became an acquaintance of Blackbeard, and developed a reputation as one of the cruelest pirates in history. Despite popular belief, Bonnet is said to be the only pirate ever to force a prisoner to walk the plank.

What would cause a responsible father and husband to cast aside a respectable life of wealth and ease? Some say the longing for adventure drove him to the sea. Others contend that he was trying to escape the critical nagging of his wife. Some believe the Major had simply gone mad.

August 1965

The elderly widow, Edna Newman, had every right to be mad (in an angry sort of way though, not in a crazy sort of way). Her entire life was being uprooted right in front of her eyes as her three children—sweating and groaning—

hoisted all of her worldly belongings from her home of 28 years into three separate U-Hauls.

But Edna wasn't mad. She was barely aware of what was going on—now or at any other time. That was actually the reason for the move.

The siblings were quite amicable as they decided who would get what. Arguments were much more likely to break out over who *had* to take something than who *got* to take something. Such was the case with the old steamer trunk, retrieved from the back of the guest bedroom closet. Its leather straps disintegrated as they dragged it across the cream-colored carpeting, and they could only hope that the rusty marks left behind were not permanent.

"If it's a treasure chest full of gold I'll take it!" one sister joked.

A second sister unclasped the latch and lifted the lid.

"A bunch of papers," she announced. "Looks like sermons or something."

"Bo-ring," sang the first.

The lid was closed again and glances exchanged until the third sibling—the lone brother—rolled his eyes and reluctantly agreed to take it.

Oblivious as they were to the fact that its contents would shed light on questions that had haunted historians for almost three centuries, the trunk was forgotten, and life went on. Eventually, however, the lid was once again opened. The treasures inside were pored over, marveled upon, and finally given to me.

The mysterious tale of Stede Bonnet, the "Gentleman Pirate," can now be told.

Some Time after, which was in August 1717, Bonnet *came off the Bar of* South-Carolina, *and took a Sloop and a Brigantine bound in; the Sloop belonged to* Barbados . . . *loaden with Rum, Sugar and Negros; and the Brigantine came from* New-England . . . *whom they plundered, and then dismiss'd; but they sail'd away with the Sloop, and at an Inlet in* North-Carolina *careened by her, and then set her on Fire.*
—*Daniel Defoe*

~ ~ ~

The Hold

It was because of the fire.

The desperate cries of the sailors had been replaying in Aaron's mind all afternoon and were the only reason he didn't hear Pell approaching the hold.

Aaron was usually quite attuned to that sound.

He turned too late to see the lanky silhouette looming in the doorway and shrank against the wall as Pell swaggered toward him, greasy hair swinging as he approached.

"Take off your shirt, boy!" the pirate said in a quiet, raspy voice, reaching for the buckle of his breeches.

It was always worse if Aaron didn't cooperate.

There was a hierarchy on the boat—a pecking order for the men to follow—and Pell was near the bottom with no one to overpower but Aaron. Experience had taught Aaron that struggling or fighting was of no use . . . the only thing for a boy of 13 to do was to escape within his mind.

But the fire had muddled not only Aaron's thoughts but his common sense, and he hesitated now. It was only for the briefest of seconds, but Pell's weathered face—hardened by cruelty and years at sea—stiffened.

Pell pulled his knife, and as the pirate strode toward him, Aaron realized in horror that Pell had taken his lack of immediate obedience as a sign of resistance or insolence. Eyes trained on the knife, Aaron struggle to explain, but his throat was as closed off as if he was already being throttled,

9

and before he could utter a word, Pell was before him, holding the knife under his chin for a long, torturous moment.

Pell leaned in and pressed the steel to the boy's throat, blowing hot breath laced with rum in his face.

"I told you to take off your shirt," Pell whispered, each word thick with the smell of alcohol and decaying teeth. "If you have a problem with that, I can do it for you."

Still unable to speak, Aaron managed to shake his head, but Pell moved the knife slowly from Aaron's throat toward his chest anyway, splaying open his shirt and the skin beneath.

The steel felt cold as it pierced Aaron's skin and sliced his flesh. He gasped in pain, then gritted his teeth as warm blood soaked his shirt. His heart pounded beneath the knife and he pressed desperately into the wall behind him. He closed his eyes, determined to take the punishment with silent resignation.

This was it.

Pell was finally going to kill him.

It wasn't the worst thing the savage pirate could do. It might be better to be killed right now than to struggle through another day of his terrorizing.

Pell ripped the bloodied shirt from Aaron's body and dropped it onto the wooden floor. Deliberately drawing out the torture, he pushed the tip of the knife into Aaron's leg, just above his knee, and slowly cut upward. Pain like bolts of white-hot lightning shot up Aaron's leg and exploded in his brain, but still he didn't cry out, though he nearly bit a hole in his lip. Once Aaron's breeches were thoroughly severed at the waist, they fell to the floor, and Aaron shivered as warm blood streamed down his leg and spattered the cloth.

A knife into my heart would be better than this slow shredding, piece by piece . . .

But suddenly the ship's captain, Bonnet, was there . . . brandishing a pistol and using it to strike Pell in the face with a bone-jarring thud. Pell's knife clattered to the floor, and Aaron wrenched free.

"Leave!" Bonnet growled, and Pell fled from the hold, cradling the side of his face with one hand.

Bonnet, his profile bony, even hawkish, holstered his weapon and stood tall and straight like the English officer he used to be. Brown hair tied neatly at the nape of his neck and his hands now clasped comfortably behind his back, Bonnet turned his attention to Aaron, who was grasping at his wounds, trying to hold the cuts together as his fingers slipped over the bloody skin.

It was a good thing Bonnet was there to help stop the bleeding . . .

But the ship's captain only spared Aaron a disdainful glance and turned away.

"Get something on," he said with disgust, and he disappeared as quickly as he had arrived.

This pirate was a gentleman of considerable fortune in the island of Barbadoes; it was therefore surprising that he should embark in such a dishonourable and dangerous undertaking. Having formed his resolution, he equipped a small vessel of ten guns and seventy men at his own expence, and in the night commenced his voyage.
—*Captain Charles Johnson*

~ ~ ~

The Black Flag

"What happened?" Bayley asked impassively, packing cloth into Aaron's leg wound.

Aaron turned his head away and closed his eyes. The viciously throbbing wound wasn't enough to block the memory of Pell.

"Don't want to talk about it, eh?"

Aaron shook his head and fought the tightening in his throat. He was never going to talk about the things Pell did to him.

Bayley wasn't usually particularly pleasant to him, but when he'd seen Aaron's condition, the sailmaster had set to work immediately, dressing his wounds.

"Probably Pell," Bayley muttered, eyeing the knife that Aaron gripped tightly in his hand. He'd retrieved Pell's weapon from the floor of the hold after Bonnet had left, and his fingers were cramped from clutching it since he'd picked it up.

Lopez and Mullet entered the room, and Aaron opened his eyes in time to see them skid to a stop and flinch, as if they'd discovered some horribly disfigured animal.

"Leave," Bayley growled. They turned to go. "And try to keep Tratt out!" he shouted after them.

"This is why someone your age shouldn't go pirating," Bayley muttered, plunging a large, threaded needle through Aaron's skin. Aaron closed his eyes again and tried to fall into blackness.

He hadn't even known that they *were* pirating until they had been at sea for several days, and by then it was too late.

Bonnet had told everyone on the island that his newly purchased ship was for the purpose of transporting sugar and rum. Aaron had vaguely noticed that there was little rum and virtually no sugar in the hold, but he'd never suspected that Bonnet was lying to everyone or that he was planning on becoming a pirate . . . why would he?

Bonnet owned a sugar plantation, and it made perfect sense that he would want to have more control over his exports. Bonnet even had a library on the ship. Who had ever heard of a pirate ship with a *library*?

The sloop was outfitted with ten cannons. Aaron had briefly wondered why they would need ten cannons, but he had other things on his mind and didn't put too much thought into it . . . until he caught sight of the flag being sewn by Bayley.

Solid black, with four white pictures: on the left there was a dagger, and on the right a heart. Parallel to the bottom, a bone filled the space and, above that, in the center, a weirdly grinning skull. Aaron knew right away that it was a pirate flag, and he finally mustered up enough courage to ask Bonnet about it.

"Every man on this ship knows why we are here," Bonnet said, "and now you do too." He smiled at Aaron—more of a sneer, really—but looked straight through him. "How long do you think it will be before everyone on that forsaken island figures it out?"

Aaron had turned on his heel and fled to the galley without answering. That "forsaken island" was his home, and apparently Bonnet had no intention of ever returning. Aaron panicked for a moment, afraid his mother would be worried about him. Then he remembered that she wouldn't.

Bonnet had christened his sloop the *Revenge*, and they'd almost immediately begun looking for ships to plunder, rapidly meeting with success. Aaron had stayed below deck in the galley during the attacks, ashamed to be a part of it all.

After the first few attacks, however, he almost convinced himself that it wasn't as terrible as he had imagined. No one had been hurt, after all, and the captured crews had been allowed to sail away on their lightened ship . . . unharmed. Barely any worse for wear.

But today, everything had changed, and there was no convincing himself that things were not terrible. After the customary two warning shots, Aaron ventured from the hold onto the deck in time to see the black flag rising up the mast, being whipsawed angrily in a cloudless sky.

Bonnet fixed his telescope on a target in the distance as the flag snapped in the wind over Aaron's head and he followed the direction of the scope to a brigantine. *I'm so sorry*, he apologized silently to the men on the ship they were approaching. *Just do whatever they say and everything will be all right.*

Bonnet spied Aaron and raised an eyebrow, sending him scurrying back below deck to cower behind a rum barrel and listen. The cannon fire thundered again, peppered with the crack of gunfire. A few commanding voices shouted orders. Other voices replied, but they were farther away and Aaron knew the pirates had boarded the other ship. More voices rose in anger but were cut short by the report of a pistol, and Aaron flinched at the sound of a grown man screaming in pain.

Soon Hart and Lopez bumped past him in the swaying hold, carrying a large trunk, followed by Dutch and Mullet, who were each hoisting large barrels.

The quartermaster, Tratt, approached Aaron and pointed to the barrels.

"Get these," he barked. Aaron nodded and leaped to his feet.

He rolled the first barrel slowly toward the hold and heard liquid sloshing inside. Aaron pressed his nose to the wood.

14

Rum.

Bayley and Dutch dumped four large bags off their shoulders into the entrance of the hold, and Aaron began struggling with the goods.

Sugar.

So the ship was transporting sugar and rum. What a coincidence; just what *they* were supposed to be doing.

The large load of rum and sugar was followed by pickled vegetables, salted meats, and spices. Aaron felt a pang of guilt as he wrestled a 50-pound sack of flour down the ladder into the hold. This wasn't what these men were *transporting*; it was what they needed for food.

"They're from Barbados," Bayley remarked to Tratt as they pushed past Aaron and climbed out of the hold.

And Aaron almost lost his grip on the sack.

As soon as he could, he climbed back up to the deck and tugged at a bag of grain, hoping to look busy. Both ships were sailing into the mouth of a river, and Aaron's eyes darted to the deck of the other ship, hoping to catch a glimpse of a familiar face from home. Aside from Pell and Vander, however, who were waving knives and swords at a small group of men, he didn't recognize anyone on board.

As Aaron stood, staring intently at the other ship, Bonnet walked by, carefully smoothing his wine-colored jacket and casting an undecipherable glance his way. Aaron dropped his eyes back to the bag and gave it an extra hard pull as Bonnet casually approached the rail.

"Mr. Pell," Bonnet called across to the other ship, "do your new friends know who I am?" Aaron couldn't miss the arrogance in his voice.

Pell grabbed one of the captive sailors by the arm and shoved him toward the rail, facing Bonnet. The man looked down, but Pell grabbed him under the chin and pointed his face in Bonnet's direction.

"Is it true you are from Barbados, sir?"

Water lapping at the boats was the only sound heard when the man did not answer. Bonnet nodded slightly at

Pell, who raised the knife and quickly pressed it to the man's throat.

"I asked if you are from Barbados, sir."

"Y-yes, yes!"

"And what is your name, sir?"

The man foolishly hesitated again and Pell drew blood. A red line trickled down the prisoner's throat.

"Your name, sir?" Bonnet asked again, his voice steady, calm, even bored.

"Palmer. Captain Joseph Palmer."

"Captain Palmer," Bonnet repeated, just loud enough to be heard. "And do you know who *I* am, Captain Palmer?"

Palmer shook his head and Bonnet laughed, a sound Aaron knew was laced with poison. "I am Major Stede Bonnet. Will you and your crew soon forget who I am?"

Palmer's eyes darted about, as if he was unsure how to answer, so he remained silent.

Bonnet glanced at Tratt. "Please make certain they don't forget." Aaron shuddered at the callousness of the verdict and the death it was about to deliver.

Bonnet turned and strode away as Tratt shouted orders to the crew and the pirates swung into violent action.

Pell shoved Palmer to the floor. Mullet and Bayley joined Vander and drew their swords, the weapons flashing like lightning. As Pell began lighting sails on fire, one man pointed a pistol at him, but Vander plunged the sword into his back before he could fire. Pell drew his own pistol and fired, causing another man to collapse. Mullet, Bayley, and Hart bounded below deck, and soon smoke was billowing from the hold.

Men scrambled for safety in opposite directions while a few jumped overboard to escape the flames. Amidst the chaos, destruction, and screams, Pell and the others returned to their ship and began swigging rum as Aaron watched the receding fire in horror.

Believing that things could not possibly get worse, Aaron tried not to listen to the fading, desperate cries of sailors as they splashed helplessly in the water. When the fire was only a small point of light on the horizon, he released himself from the punishment of watching the drama and fled back to the hold . . .

And that was where he had stayed. Until Pell found him.

Another plunge of Bayley's needle into his thigh brought Aaron back to the here and now. He felt nauseated and tried to roll over, but Bayley held him down.

"Stay still or you'll keep bleeding," the makeshift doctor ordered, reaching past Aaron's head for a piece of cloth.

Aaron smelled the smoke on Bayley's clothes and hair from the earlier fire and let out a quavering breath. The sights and sounds of the fire were still with him, and now the smell was too. The scent was as powerful as the men's screams of agony that were somehow still ringing in his ears.

Why?

On many occasions, Bonnet had elaborated about his hatred of his grandmother: "an old witch" who cared about nothing more than "impressing the courtiers." Aaron knew this was why Bonnet had wanted to make such a memorable impression on the men from Barbados—what better way to seek revenge on his grandmother than to disgrace the very family name of which she was so proud?

But why did it have to be fire?

Aaron would have thought that the family name had already been disgraced enough. Hadn't the woman been thoroughly humiliated by the fact that Bonnet had inexplicably left not only her but his wife and three children as well? Aaron had seen the children on the island from time to time (although they never paid any attention to him). He wondered now if Bonnet worried about the fact that he was disgracing *their* family name as well, and he wondered if Bonnet cared about them at all, or if he ever thought about how they were feeling.

But Aaron was fairly certain he knew the answer to that: Bonnet had only cared for one person in his entire life, and it wasn't one of his children.

"You'd better stop getting Pell mad at you," Bayley said, ripping a piece of cloth and bringing Aaron back to the present yet again. "Of course if Tratt takes over he'll probably rein everyone in a mite better."

Takes over?

"What do you mean?" Aaron managed to ask through a tight, dry throat.

Bayley shrugged as his hands skillfully wrapped Aaron's wounds. "Well, it might not be Tratt, could be Mullet or even Dutch. Hard to say right now. But it's just a matter of time before someone else is put in charge."

"But . . ." Aaron blinked. "But Bonnet pays us—we work for him."

"You can't *hire* pirates," Bayley said, peering over his little silver spectacles. "Bonnet thinks he can, but he doesn't know anything about us. Doesn't know anything about sailing either. It's just a matter of time."

"But—" Aaron cut himself off when he saw the older man's face change.

Bayley rubbed his wild white beard and frowned at the blood seeping through the fresh dressing on Aaron's chest.

"I'm just telling you what I know," Bayley said, repacking the wound, "and if I were you, I'd find a way to stay away from Pell."

Aaron had been *trying* stay away from Pell since the first day they'd met, but Pell kept finding him.

"Best I can do," Bayley eventually announced, slapping his knees with finality. He rose and blew out the lantern as he left.

Aaron renewed his grip on Pell's knife, grasping it tightly in the dark, and ignored the throbs of pain from his gashes as he tried to figure out what to do. He didn't really have any options, but he kept searching anyway, no longer foolish enough to believe that things couldn't get any worse.

He was certain that if things *did* get worse, he wasn't going to survive.

*On board the Pirate Sloop is Major Bonnet, but has no
Command, he walks about in his Morning Gown, and then to his
Books, of which he has a good Library on Board, he was not well of
his wounds that he received by attacking of a Spanish Man of War,
which kill'd and wounded him 30 or 40 Men.*
— *Captain Codd, 1717*

~ ~ ~

Scars

As Aaron's deep cuts turned into wide, red scars, it
became very apparent that what Bayley had said was true—
the men were growing unhappy with Bonnet. Despite the
fact that Bonnet paid them regularly, Aaron often heard
them muttering about his incompetence or the need to
replace him. The crew didn't mind voicing their discontent
in front of Aaron as he swabbed the deck or mended nets.
Evil winds led them about the Atlantic Ocean, capturing
ship after ship and listening more and more to each other
rather than to Bonnet.

The steady pay provided by Bonnet, however,
apparently appeased the men sufficiently to keep them
from following through with their grumbled threats—at
least it did until one morning when Aaron was jarred awake
by the thunderous boom of cannons firing.

That sound—in and of itself—wasn't so unusual, but
the muffled boom of return fire was. Aaron raced to the
deck and found Bonnet and Pell standing at the rail,
watching a ship that was dangerously close. Tratt, a few feet
away on the command deck, carefully maneuvered the
captain's wheel. The sloop they approached was not
surrendering to the black flag and customary warning shot
as usually happened.

"Closer!" Bonnet barked.

"Tratt thinks they're too heavily armed," Pell replied,
resting his hand on the butt of his gun. "We need to hang
back."

"Tratt is not in command of this—"

Bonnet's diatribe was cut short as the *Revenge* was hit with a blast. The ship rocked and Aaron grabbed hold of the mizzenmast for support. Nearby, Dutch fell to the deck, blood squirting from his chest. Several of the men standing nearby traded uneasy glances with Pell.

"Closer! Closer!" Bonnet yelled at Tratt, his neck and face turning red.

Pell leaned over Dutch, although clearly there was nothing to be done for him.

"Leave him!" Bonnet bellowed at Pell and the other men as they inched a bit closer. They ignored him and continued to stare at Dutch's body, tearing their gaze away only long enough to look at one another.

Bonnet pulled his pistol. "You'll do as I say!" he shouted, leveling his weapon at Pell. The men retreated, but Aaron saw the hatred in their eyes.

Suddenly Vander, climbing in the rigging of the sails, fell to the deck with a loud thud as the *Revenge* took another hit. Neither Bonnet nor Pell looked away from each other as the hand rolled on the deck, moaning in pain and clutching his bloodied arm.

"Go!" Tratt shouted to Hart, pointing to the spot in the rigging where Vander had been.

Bonnet wheeled around to point his pistol at Tratt.

"You'll not give the orders on my ship!" Bonnet growled.

"I *will* give the orders since you don't know what you're doing!" Tratt replied, skirting the wheel and heading straight toward Bonnet. "You're going to get us all—"

Bonnet fired his pistol at Tratt's face. A shower of blood exploded out of the back of his head and the quartermaster dropped to the deck, his face mangled and unrecognizable.

Almost before the sailor hit the deck, Bonnet snatched another pistol from his waist and pointed it at Pell. The sailor's face change to ash gray as Bonnet slowly turned to look at Aaron and order, "Get to the galley."

Aaron didn't understand at first that the command was for him. He stared in disbelief for a moment, first at Pell and then at Tratt's lifeless body. Tratt's face was a bloody stew of red meat and bone. Raked by a quick, cold stare from Bonnet, Aaron swallowed hard and headed below deck.

Pacing in the galley under the thunder of cannons and screams, Aaron's heart pounded in his chest. When the noise finally ceased with an ominous abruptness, he cautiously returned to the deck above. Blood, dead pirates, body parts, and wounded men—moaning in agony— littered the deck. Walking through the field of human debris, Aaron tried to numb himself against the mangled and bloody bodies, the desperate groans, and the smell of smoke and death.

Bayley motioned to him to help pick up Vander, who was groaning in pain. Finding no part that wasn't covered in blood, they grabbed hold anyway and dragged the large, shredded man to his bunk and then headed above deck again. As they emerged from the hold, Aaron saw Hart and Lopez dump a lifeless Tratt over the rail with all the sentimentality of gulls who discard the bones of a meal. He quickly turned his attention to helping Bayley, but the image of Tratt's body unceremoniously disappearing over the rail wouldn't leave him.

On Bayley's order, Aaron used all the strength and weight of his young frame to pin down an injured man while a piece of wood was dislodged from his shoulder. Once the chunk had been fished out, Aaron helped the man to his feet and led him below to a bunk near Vander.

When Aaron arrived above deck again, he saw Bayley crouching over Pell. Blood had soaked through his shirt near his shoulder and through his pants above his knee. The stains grew as Aaron watched.

"Is he dead?" he asked, trying not to sound hopeful.

"No, he's breathing."

They struggled to lift him as crew members hoisted more bodies over the rail. Bonnet was unconscious, too, and they moved him next. Aaron and his shipmates made trip after gory trip and soon he was drenched in blood, not a drop of it his own. By the time all the wounded men were taken below deck and all the dead stripped of their clothing and thrown into the ocean, full dark had settled on the ship.

"Here's some more cloth," Aaron said, handing the fresh dressings to Bayley. Deep into the night, their shadows flickered on the ship's curved walls. They had just finished mending Bonnet's deep leg wound and a less serious bullet graze above his brow.

"Cut his clothes off," Bayley said, pointing to Pell, who was still unconscious.

Aaron hesitated, but then cautiously approached Pell and pulled out his knife. Actually it was Pell's knife. Aaron lifted the cloth from Pell's chest and cut his shirt gingerly, as if a sudden movement might rouse him. Exposing Pell's chest and belly, Aaron peeled back the blood-soaked shirt, held the lantern over him, and sucked in his breath.

There was blood, yes—a wound near his shoulder kept pumping out a small trickle—but Aaron had seen blood and wounds before. What shocked him were the scars. *Dozens* of them—in all shapes and size. They covered Pell's torso. Aaron quickly cut off Pell's breeches and found more of the same, shining white through the fresh blood smeared on his legs.

Aaron was still staring at Pell when Bayley approached.

"What's it look like?" Bayley asked.

"I . . . I don't know," Aaron said.

Bayley examined the shoulder wound first and pushed Pell onto his side to see that the bullet had exited cleanly. Aaron saw even more scars on Pell's back. Bayley didn't seem to notice at all.

"How did he get all those scars?" Aaron finally asked after Bayley had firmly packed a wad of cloth against Pell's shoulder.

Bayley glanced down at Pell's body and then shrugged, but Aaron was too enthralled to let it drop. He slid the lantern's handle over a hook and asked again. "What happened? Was he in a fight?"

"Probably not," Bayley said, taking another strip of cloth from Aaron's hands. "I'm guessing he got 'em a few at a time."

Bayley dug skillfully into the leg wound to search for shrapnel. Pell suddenly opened his eyes, sat bolt upright, and locked eyes with Aaron, whose face was only inches from Pell's. With hardly a hitch in his doctoring, Bayley shoved Pell back down where he immediately passed out again, but Aaron could barely breathe.

"I'm going to get some more cloth," Aaron managed, and he raced away.

Riffling through the clothes they'd taken off Dutch's body, looking for something Bayley could use for dressing, Aaron felt an unexpected wave of sympathy for Pell. At some point in his miserable life, Pell had been beaten, stabbed, burned, and torn. Maybe when he was Aaron's age—perhaps even younger.

But then Aaron stopped digging for cloth and sat back, touching his chest with one hand and his leg with the other. His own scars were still tender, the skin uncomfortably tight.

Any feelings of sympathy he had disappeared. He scooted over to Tratt's things and began digging for bandages there.

He derived this name from his long, black beard, which, like a frightful meteor, covered his whole face, and terrified America more than any comet that had ever appeared. He was accustomed to twist it with ribbon in small quantities resembling those of some fashionable wigs, and turn them about his ears. In time of action he wore a sling over his shoulders with three brace of pistols. He stuck lighted matches under his hat, which appearing on both sides of his face and his eyes, naturally fierce and wild, made him such a figure that the human imagination cannot form a conception of even a fury more terrible and alarming; and if he had the appearance and look of a fury, his actions corresponded with that character.

—Captain Charles Johnson

~ ~ ~

Rosalie

Of the men who did not die, Bonnet was one of the more seriously wounded. He thrashed in his bunk, feverish and delirious for over two weeks, and when his fever finally did break he could barely move without excruciating pain. He barked a few feeble orders from his bunk and tried to venture above deck to resume command, but in reality he could not even stand straight for very long and a pained look etched deep lines in his face.

Meanwhile, Pell recovered quite nicely, and Mullet unofficially took over command of the ship. He ordered that the *Revenge*—greatly in need of repairs—sail up the Cape Fear River to careen.

The crew steered her into waters that were shallow but still affected by the ebb and flow of the ocean. They set up camp on the shore near the anchored ship. As the tides went out, the ship would list severely to one side or the other, leaving a large section of her hull dry and exposed. The men would then have several hours to work on the repairs before the waters returned, righting her once again.

After the deaths of so many, the workload on each man increased dramatically and Mullet ordered Aaron over the side of the ship almost every day to scrape barnacles while other crew members replaced broken boards or patched the sides with pitch. The men fended for themselves, finding whatever food they could scrounge from the hold.

From below deck, Bonnet sent word that he wanted to sail north. Aaron picked and scraped at the razor-sharp barnacles on the ship's sides and listened to the crew topside grumble about the order.

"He wants to go to Boston," Aaron heard Bayley tell Mullet.

"We're going to Honduras," Mullet replied.

Bayley nodded. "I told him how the crew had voted, but you know how he is."

"I reckon he'll learn soon enough," Mullet said.

When the day finally came that Bonnet was able to hoist himself up the ladder and venture on deck, the ship had already been repaired and the men were sailing toward the Bay of Honduras. Apparently Bonnet had either changed his mind about sailing north or he sensed that the men were not going to obey his orders, because he behaved as if this new destination was his idea. When he continued paying them regularly, Aaron wondered if Bonnet actually believed he was still in charge.

The Bay of Honduras turned out to be a haven for pirates and privateers of the Atlantic coast, and it wasn't long after the *Revenge* arrived there that her men were socializing with the crews of other ships anchored nearby. It was not unusual for the men to climb aboard another ship and spend hours there—eating, drinking, bragging of the women they'd met in the last port or those they'd find in the next, and trying to outdo one another in various battles of strength and wit.

Taking some food into Bonnet's cabin one day, Aaron was startled to find a dark, menacing figure seated across from the captain.

"They're taking advantage of me," Bonnet told the large, burly man in a hushed voice. "They know that I'm weak and that I cannot command as I once did."

Dressed all in black, the man tugged at his bushy charcoal beard and nodded knowingly, glancing up as Aaron set the food in front of Bonnet.

"Shall I bring another serving?" Aaron asked, looking first to Bonnet and then to the man.

"No," the man said, rising from his seat and towering over Aaron. "I'll speak with Hornigold." He strode out the door of the cabin.

"Anything else?" Aaron asked Bonnet.

"They think that they can get rid of me?" Bonnet muttered, more to himself than to Aaron. "They think they can elect another to take command of *my* ship?"

Aaron stayed quiet. Bonnet gestured toward the man who had just left.

"If Hornigold lets Blackbeard command my ship, you'd best get ready for some changes, my boy," Bonnet growled, reaching for the bowl. "Get ready for some changes."

As it turned out, Hornigold did give permission for Blackbeard to captain the *Revenge* until Bonnet was healthy again. Aaron seriously doubted that restored health would be enough to return command to Bonnet, but he kept those thoughts to himself, and—as Bonnet had predicted—changes did indeed occur.

Blackbeard brought the crew of the *Revenge* under swift control. He had a knack for determining what every man should do on the ship, and after he assigned them each to their positions, the entire tone on the ship changed.

A man named Lieutenant Richards was brought over from Hornigold's ship and named quartermaster, second in command only to Blackbeard himself. Hart, promoted to sailing master, took charge of navigation, and Mullet replaced him as gunner, the position responsible for the cannons, powder supplies, and the heavy armaments. As the new boatswain, Pell would handle all the ship's maintenance.

It seemed that Pell was eager to please Blackbeard. Swaggering with pride over his newfound authority, he stayed surprisingly occupied. Perhaps because Pell was so busy with his new position (or maybe because he was afraid of Blackbeard), Aaron was left largely alone. Bonnet stayed in his quarters, continuing to recuperate, and Aaron went back to working in the galley.

Other members of Hornigold's crew wound up joining Blackbeard aboard the *Revenge*. Aaron's favorite—by far—was Husk.

Husk had dark weathered skin and gray thinning hair. He was a large, round man, his blue eyes always shining with a friendly light. Aaron wondered repeatedly how such a jovial man had fallen into the dark life of a pirate. He played the violin as well as anyone Aaron had ever heard, and whenever night fell and Husk started to play, Aaron ventured above deck to listen. Although much of what Husk played was jovial if not raucous, some of the tunes were beautiful and downright enchanting. Even the most boisterous of pirates would settle down and listen peacefully when Husk played "Greensleeves."

As much as he loved the music, the thing Aaron liked best about Husk was Rosalie. Rosalie was Husk's macaw—a large, brilliant red bird with bright amber eyes that seemed to follow Aaron wherever he went.

Husk ventured into the galley often, sometimes bringing fresh meat for Aaron to cook for the crew, sometimes just coming to visit, but always bringing Rosalie. He let Aaron hold her, feed her, and pet her, and Aaron was glad that both of them were now on the ship.

Sometimes Husk would leave Rosalie with Aaron in the galley and come to pick her up a few hours later. Awed by the bird's bright colors and intelligence, Aaron thought she was wonderful and never tired of watching after her. Husk entered the galley one day without her and Aaron was immediately alarmed.

"Where's Rosalie?" he asked.

"Oh, I left her in her cage for a time."

"Oh," Aaron said, clearly disappointed.

"Don't worry, you'll have plenty of opportunity to see her."

"I will?"

"Yes indeed, you will." Husk nodded. "Hornigold's going his own way and me and a few others are staying on to help Blackbeard—that is, if you don't mind the company." Husk winked and Aaron smiled.

As Hornigold prepared to go his own way, the combined crews captured a huge four-masted, square-rigged ship named the *Concorde*. Although pirates usually preferred to sail in small, fast ships, Blackbeard decided to keep her and, after Hornigold sailed away, he divided his crew between the two remaining ships. He named his new ship the *Queen Anne's Revenge*, sent Lieutenant Richards to command her, and—to Aaron's delight—sent Pell to work on the new ship as well. Aaron was even more delighted to find that Husk was assigned to stay on the *Revenge*.

Husk and Rosalie were staying . . . Pell was leaving. It wasn't a bad trade.

The two ships sailed north, cautiously prowling the Atlantic waters. Although Aaron still slept with his hand wrapped around the knife every night, the weeks passed and he hardly saw Pell. They captured tremendous numbers of ships and—although Aaron dreaded each attack—there was usually very little violence. Men seeing the black flags flying on the two approaching ships usually surrendered peacefully and were set free after their cargo was taken. Some men even chose to join with the pirates . . . the numbers on the ships increased and their success continued.

Life was almost good.

One day Aaron found himself softly humming a happy tune as he chopped up some wilted cabbage and smiled at his mood.

"You wanna put this in the salmagundi?" Husk asked as he strode into the galley, handing over some fresh sea bass for the stew.

Aaron nodded. He set the fish in the dry sink and then reached into a sack for a piece of hardtack. Clamping his teeth down on the bread, Aaron struggled to break it.

"Where'd you get Rosalie?" Aaron asked, hoping the loud crack he heard wasn't a tooth. He handed the piece he'd bitten off to Rosalie.

"Rosalie?" Husk said, reaching up and smoothing her feathers. "Took her off a ship near Port Royal."

"I wish I had a pet," Aaron said, rubbing his jaw. Rosalie dropped a large crumb on the floor and turned one bright eye to it.

"Oh, Rosalie ain't a pet," Husk said.

"She's not?" Aaron stooped to pick up the crumb for her.

"No," Husk shook his head. "I'm going to sell her."

Aaron's eyes widened at the news. He fed the crumb to Rosalie and asked softly, "Who are you going to sell her to?"

"Whoever's willing to pay," Husk said. "Timberhead sold one to some dame in London last year for over ten pounds!"

"How much do you want?" Aaron asked, quickly trying to calculate how much he could pay.

"Oh, no sir. I know what you're thinkin'. You don't want her, trust me."

"But—"

"I know it probably seems like a splendid idea to have a pet, but you can't take care of a bird proper-like on a ship."

"I—"

"She makes a mess all the time—" Husk interrupted, jerking his thumb over his shoulder. "Usually down my

30

back . . . she squawks whenever she goes into her cage . . . always worrying about her if we get fired on . . . trust me, you don't want her."

Oh, but Aaron *did* want her.

It didn't take him long to convince Husk to sell Rosalie. Aaron had all his salary he'd earned from Bonnet during the months since they'd set sail, in addition to the money he'd left Barbados with. Husk greedily eyed Aaron's cupped hands, filled with coins, and handed Rosalie over, cage and all.

Aaron worried that she would pine for Husk, but Rosalie never looked back. It seemed as though she knew she was his, as if she understood that he had given everything he owned for her and as if she appreciated the gesture.

Each morning she anxiously clacked her beak up and down the bars of her cage until Aaron let her out, and then she would willingly do whatever he asked of her. If Aaron put her on a perch, she stayed there and watched him intently. If he extended his hand to her, she climbed on. She gingerly took food from his hand, apparently aware that her beak held the power to snap off a finger if she wasn't careful. Her nips on his ear when she rode his shoulder were so gentle that he decided she must be trying to tickle him and he always laughed, hoping to humor her.

Whenever he entered the hold now, it was with his knife in one hand, a lantern in the other, and Rosalie riding on his shoulder; three things to protect him from whomever he might find—or whoever might find him.

The only problem with her was that Husk had been right—she *was* messy. Cracked seeds and dried feces littered the floor under her cage, feathers settled into the stew, and his shirt required a fresh washing almost daily. But Aaron never complained about this—not even inwardly. He felt privileged to have her and couldn't resent anything about her. Instead, he cleaned up after her diligently, constantly making sure that she gave none of the crew reason to complain or object to him having her.

While Aaron clawed a little joy out of his unique existence, the *Revenge* and the *Queen Anne's Revenge* sailed along the Atlantic coast together capturing ship after ship and increasing the fortune of their crews. It seemed that the men were too happy and content to bother complaining about the young cook and his bird.

Aaron could scarcely believe his good fortune—things in his life were finally good. No, he wasn't living the life of a choir boy surrounded by saints, but he was grateful for simple pleasures. Not only did he have Rosalie, but Pell hadn't been aboard the *Revenge* in weeks.

Aaron was happy. He was finally happy.

He should have known it wouldn't last.

But Pirates prey upon all Mankind, their own Species and
Fellow-Creatures, without Distinction of Nations or Religions;
English, French, Spaniards, and Portuguese, and Moors
and Turks, *are all alike to them: for Pirates are not content with*
taking from the Merchants what Things they stand in need of, but
throw their Goods over-board, burn their ships, and sometimes bereave
them of their Lives for Pastime and Diversion . . .
—*Richard Allein, 1718*

~ ~ ~

Optimism

They say that your earliest memory can tell a lot about
you—whether you tend to have a happy outlook on life or
not, whether you tend to be an optimist or a pessimist. If
your first memory is pleasant or happy, you are most likely
an optimist. If your first memory is disturbing or
uncomfortable, you are probably a pessimist. If this is true,
then Aaron was an optimist. His first memory was of
sitting in a sugar cane field, holding a stalk longer than he
was and sucking the sweet liquid from one end. It was a
short memory, but definitely a happy one. Yes, Aaron was
likely an optimist.

He was certainly feeling optimistic now. Down in the
galley, a dark, cramped space, Aaron chopped meat for
stew and caught himself humming again. This time, the
tune was no random ditty. His mother had taught him the
song one afternoon as they'd strung together herbs to hang
from the rafters. She had been dead for nine months now,
and Aaron realized this was the first time that the thought
of her didn't bring a stabbing pain.

"You know," Aaron said to Rosalie as he scraped the
meat into a boiling broth, "I might just make some fresh
bread if I can get some leavening. My mother used to make
it all the time . . . I think I could do it. Don't you think
everyone would like that for a change instead of hardtack?"

Content on her perch, Rosalie lifted one foot to the
side of her face and scratched.

"Come here," he said gently, setting down his knife and holding out his arm to her. She stepped onto his hand as Husk entered the galley.

"Salmagundi again, eh?" Husk asked, peering into the cauldron.

"Sorry," Aaron said. "We haven't had a lot of variety lately, have we? I was just telling Rosalie that I might make some fresh bread if I can buy some yeast."

"You'll stock up good in Havana," Husk said.

"We're going to Havana?"

"*You* are," Husk said. "I'm going with Blackbeard."

The announcement caused a sinking feeling in Aaron's gut. "Blackbeard's *leaving*?"

"Certainly is. Bonnet's up and about now and Blackbeard's got a beautiful new ship of his own ... he's taking his *Queen Anne's Revenge* and sailing to St. Thomas. Your crew wants to go to Havana."

Absently, Aaron put Rosalie back on her perch. Blackbeard's departure wasn't good. Aaron didn't want to think about how Pell was going to start behaving if the notorious pirate left.

"But Bonnet has been wanting to go to Boston," Aaron said, trying to push those thoughts from his mind. "Why are we going to Havana?"

Husk paused before answering, one eyebrow diving down. "How long you been sailin' with Bonnet?"

Aaron hadn't really been counting the days. Rosalie flapped her wings and shook her head.

"I don't know," he finally shrugged, "maybe half of a year?"

Husk nodded.

"Why?"

"Have you ever noticed that he's a bit . . . um . . ."

"A bit what?" Aaron took a cautious step toward the only man on the ship he would call a friend.

"Um . . ." Husk didn't quite seem to know what to say. That was one of the things he liked most about Husk—he was the only *polite* pirate Aaron had ever met.

34

Entertaining as it was to watch Husk struggle for a way to describe Bonnet and be nice at the same time, Aaron finally decided to help him out. "Incompetent?" he suggested.

Husk smiled, pulling his shoulders back. "Well, I was going to say odd. How'd he ever get elected captain, anyway?"

"It's his boat," Aaron said, turning toward Rosalie to stroke her feathers. "He hired us."

"Oh . . ."

Aaron sighed and looked at Husk. "They're talking about getting rid of him again aren't they?"

Husk nodded.

"You can come with us," Husk offered.

"No," Aaron said quietly. "I'm staying."

"Blackbeard's not so bad . . . he runs a tight ship, but he's smart—you'll get your share of a lot more sailing with Blackbeard."

Aaron shook his head.

"Well," Husk said, "Suit yourself, but I think if you stay on this ship you'll be seeing Havana a lot sooner than you see Boston, no matter what Bonnet desires."

As Blackbeard and Bonnet prepared to part ways, a large number of men from the *Revenge* decided to permanently join Blackbeard's crew on the *Queen Anne's Revenge*, and Aaron was elated when he learned that Pell was one of those men. Wiggling happily in his bunk, Aaron enjoyed feeling really safe for the first time in months.

"Pell's leaving," he told Rosalie quietly, the night before Blackbeard sailed away. "Can you believe it? We're going to be completely free of him!"

He gripped his knife loosely and ran one finger idly along the back side of the blade. Tomorrow night he wouldn't even need it. So pleased that he could barely fall asleep, he closed his eyes and waited, aware that he had a silly grin pasted on his face. Aaron suspected it would still be there in the morning.

Not long after sunrise, Aaron stood at the rail and watched the *Queen Anne's Revenge* bob in the water as the crew hoisted her anchor.

Good riddance, he thought, spying Pell on the deck of the departing ship.

As if he'd heard Aaron's thoughts, Pell turned to face the *Revenge* and walked to the rail, standing directly opposite Aaron. Stringy, gray hair blowing in the wind, he grabbed the rail with weathered hands and leaned toward Aaron. His baleful glare radiated hatred.

Aaron's initial instinct urged him to back away and escape Pell's smoldering stare, but instead he took a deep breath and stood his ground.

He can't hurt me anymore, Aaron thought. *Let him stand there and stare at me all he wants.*

Wind filled the sails of the *Queen Anne's Revenge* and she started drifting away. Aaron and Pell continued staring at each other for several more seconds before Pell reached down and pulled something from his belt. He raised the object just slightly above the rail, as if hiding it from the other pirates.

Startled, Aaron thought Pell was reaching for a pistol but soon realized it wasn't a weapon. He squinted. Something small and red. He stared at the red thing, trying to figure out what it was, but his brain just wouldn't make a connection. Pell raised it a bit higher and twirled it deliberately in his fingers.

A slow, ugly smile parted his lips.

And with a sudden jolt, Aaron realized Pell was holding a *feather*. A bright red feather.

He tore down to the hold and raced to Rosalie's cage.

Her perch sat empty. Red feathers littered the bottom of her cage and the floor below.

A wave of sadness engulfed him, followed by an upwelling of rage, and his throat tightened to near suffocation as he reached into the cage and picked up a large feather. Aaron ran his fingers over it and then rubbed it against his cheek. He clamped his teeth together to try to stop the pain from getting past his throat, but it was unstoppable. It seeped to his eyes and escaped in the form of one tear that rolled down his right cheek.

Silently, methodically, he gathered up all the feathers and put them on the floor of the cage. Moving with the forlorn stiffness of a pallbearer, he carried all of it above deck and crossed to the rail. The *Queen Anne's Revenge* was only a dark speck on the horizon now.

Aaron hoisted the cage over his head and, growling, flung it toward the ship with all his might. He watched as it tumbled into the water, followed by a crimson trail of twisting, fluttering feathers.

One feather had fallen to the deck. He leaned down, picked it up, held it tightly for a moment, and then reached his hand over the rail and unfolded his fingers. He didn't stay to watch as it drifted on the sea breeze down into the turquoise waters.

Thou shalt not make thee any grave image, or any likeness of any thing that is in heaven above, or that is in the earth beneath, or that is in the waters beneath the earth. Thou shalt not bow down thyself unto them, nor serve them: for I the Lord thy God am a jealous God, visiting the iniquity of the fathers upon the children unto the third and fourth generation of them that hate me.
—Deuteronomy 5:8–9

~ ~ ~

The Darkest Days

It was wintertime, and although Aaron was fairly certain that Bonnet still wanted to sail north along the eastern coast of America, they stayed in the warmer waters as Husk had predicted. They sailed to Nassau on New Providence Island, visited Port Royal, and went to Havana. Each port was a popular destination for pirates but Aaron—apprehensive that he may run into Pell if he went ashore at any one of them—stayed on board the ship.

The crew, however, was anxious to spend their money. Between visiting ports, they captured numerous ships and acquired an abundance of booty. On the islands, there was no shortage of ways to spend the newly acquired wealth. The men raucously squandered their money on food, drinks, and women.

Aaron had no interest in any of it. Even if he'd had the slightest desire to join in, his heart would not have been in it. Ever since *Queen Anne's Revenge* had sailed away, his thoughts darkened and nothing pleasant would come to his mind. He went about his chores quietly, almost trance-like.

No. There was *one* ray of sunshine: Pell was finally gone. Aaron kept this thought in the forefront of his mind and held on to it as if it was a lifeline—the one thought that could keep him from sliding into an inescapable pit of bitterness.

While they were at sea, Aaron's duties in the galley kept him mercifully busy; however, whenever the *Revenge* reached a port and the men raced ashore, his workload dwindled to nearly nothing. Aaron found himself with very little to do besides whittle and watch the crowds on the dock.

Though exhausted, he slept fitfully at night now and the knife returned to his hand. Dreams of blood and feathers and Pell haunted what sleep he did find. Mostly, though, he lay awake, staring at the ship's wall next to his bunk and listening to the restless ship. Those were the times Aaron dreaded the most. In these dark hours, he revisited the events of the past year over and over.

On some level, he understood that everything that had happened to him had been out of his control from the very beginning. Another part of him, though, wondered if there was something he could have done differently to have changed the course that had brought him to this ship.

Why was this happening to him? Was God punishing him—and if so—for what? He wasn't without sin, he knew that. But what could he have *possibly* done to deserve this?

One night, when those thoughts were running particularly wild through his mind and holding sleep at bay, Aaron rose from his bunk and soon found himself in Bonnet's library. He swung his lantern across the shelves of books until he found a copy of the Bible. He slid it out and returned to his bunk, doubting Bonnet would ever miss it.

He spent night after night, perusing the pages of the Bible, trying to determine why God had allowed these things to happen to him, flipping randomly to a different spot each night and reading.

One night, anchored off the coast of Havana, Aaron was reading from Exodus:

Thou shalt not make unto thee any graven image, or any likeness of any thing that is in heaven above, or that is in the earth beneath, or that is in the water under the earth. Thou shalt not bow down thyself to them, nor serve them . . .

He was fairly confident he hadn't broken that one. He continued reading.

. . . for I the Lord thy God am a jealous God, visiting the iniquity of the fathers upon the children unto the third and fourth generation of them that hate me . . .

His heart began pounding and he read it again.

Visiting the iniquity of the fathers upon the children to the third and fourth generation . . .

And suddenly he understood.

It wasn't his fault—it was his *father's* fault. He was being rebuked for the sins of his father.

He was being punished for something that he hadn't even done.

His children would be punished . . . his grandchildren . . .

And Aaron decided right then and there that he was never going to have children.

He wasn't going to be responsible for someone else enduring a life of hardship like the one he was living. He didn't wish that on anybody, especially his own children.

Over the next few days, however, a calm satisfaction settled over Aaron. Now that he understood *why* he was going through these trials, they were somehow easier to bear.

And most of all, he found a distinct peace in knowing that none of this was his fault.

In the early spring, the crew voted to sail back to the Bay of Honduras.

They were not far from their destination when they spotted a mercantile ship, and just after dark, Bonnet ordered that the ship be fired upon.

It didn't take long before Aaron was jolted with the realization that cannons were firing back at the *Revenge*. No ship had dared return fire since the early days when Tratt and Dutch had been killed, and—more than a little concerned—Aaron climbed above deck and crouched behind two giant stacks of anchor rope to watch the fighting.

The ship they had attacked was obviously very well armed for a merchant ship—even in the dark this much was quite apparent. She belched fire, unloading upon the *Revenge* relentlessly and even hitting it occasionally, but the crew managed to keep out of range for the most part.

During a lull, Bonnet approached the rail. Looking like a ghost washed in silver moonlight, he raised his speaking trumpet and addressed the captain of the other ship.

"Surrender peacefully," he called, "or you shall suffer great consequences."

Aaron thought he heard the slightest waver in Bonnet's voice and his request was answered with a deafening barrage of thundering, flashing explosions.

"They're not going to surrender," Mullet said after almost an hour of fighting. Clearly frustrated, several members of the crew had formed a half-circle around him and Bonnet at the wheel. The *Revenge* had continued to manage to stay far enough away to avoid much damage, but neither were they any closer to taking the prize.

"We can take them," Vander insisted, edging forward. The crew seemed to agree. They'd become so used to taking whatever they wanted that they were now unwilling to retreat. Bonnet nodded his agreement and the men scrambled to launch another assault.

When Aaron shifted in his hiding place, Bonnet spotted him and ordered him below deck. He scuttled down to the galley in a hurry and from there listened to continual firing from both ships until, finally, the crew of the *Revenge* gave up and sailed away.

In the morning, Bonnet tried to address the crew, but they were angry and blamed him for their rare defeat.

Arguing with raised fists and puffed-up chests, the crew was impatient, and possibly dangerous. When Mullet called for a vote to continue on their current course, Bonnet stood stoic and silent. He didn't argue, nor did he counter-command the vote.

Aaron saw the defeat in his eyes.

Within a few days they reached the Bay of Honduras, and as they approached the Turneffe Islands, the summer sun shimmered like diamonds on the water. Aaron didn't recall the water at Barbados ever looking so deep, so dream-like. As the *Revenge* sailed into harbor, he shielded his eyes from the sun and noted the other pirate ships sailing out. Several of them looked ready and willing to take advantage of any poorly armed merchant vessels that might have the misfortune to pass by.

As he headed down to the galley, Aaron heard the men above deck whooping and hollering, obviously acknowledging the crew of a ship they recognized.

He riffled through the hold for some vegetables and when he returned to the galley, arms full, he could still hear the noises from above—in fact the racket seemed to be growing in intensity. Aaron set the potatoes and beans down in a dry sink and ventured above deck to investigate. He recognized the flag before he reached the rail.

Even from a good distance, as the *Queen Anne's Revenge* sailed up beside them—looming like an evil shadow— Aaron felt Pell's stare before he saw him.

. . . Teach, finding that Bonnet knew nothing of a maritime Life, with the Consent of his own Men, put in another Captain, one Richards, to command Bonnet's Sloop, and took the Major on aboard his own Ship, telling him, that as he had not been used to the Fatigues and Care of such a Post, it would be better for him to decline it, to live easy, at his Pleasure, in such a Ship as his, where he would not be obliged to perform the necessary Duties of a Sea Voyager.
—Daniel Defoe

~ ~ ~

Sailing with Blackbeard Again

Aaron not only kept his knife on his person now, he pulled it out whenever he entered the hold. He fully expected to see Pell leap from the shadows at any moment. Although Pell showed no inclination to leave the *Queen Anne's Revenge*, the ship was anchored only a stone's throw away and that was too close for Aaron.

At least Husk started paying regular visits again, and he played the violin on one ship or the other most nights. It was good to see him once more, as Aaron had missed his twinkling eyes and kind manners. Husk never asked about Rosalie, but Aaron suspected he already knew—Pell had probably bragged about it to everyone on board the *Queen Anne's Revenge*.

"Did you go to Havana?" Husk asked casually one day as he tweaked and plucked his fiddle in preparation of an evening's entertainment.

Aaron nodded.

"Did you like it?"

Aaron shrugged.

"Well, you're still kinda young. A few more years and you'll probably enjoy it a lot more." Aaron nodded, but he doubted it. No matter how old he was, he didn't think he would ever enjoy what the raucous ports had to offer. "Well, warmer weather's coming," Husk continued. "Maybe Bonnet will finally get to Boston."

"Maybe."

"He doin' any better as captain?" Husk asked.

"Not really. Everyone's pretty angry at him. He's still paying us, but I think that's the only thing that's kept him from being replaced. No one listens to him anymore . . . Mullet seems to be in charge."

Husk was putting the violin to his neck but stopped. "And how do you feel regarding that?"

Aaron pondered the question for a moment and then told Husk how he really felt: "I could barely care less."

Husk nodded and put his fiddle and bow in position, but Aaron reached out and stopped him.

"Husk?"

He looked up, old blue eyes wary.

"Husk," Aaron asked, "why do you do this?"

"Do what?"

"This . . ." Aaron indicated the ship. " . . . Pirating."

"I'm a seaman, boy! It's in my blood. Ain't no other place for me."

"But why not just be a regular seaman—one who gets paid? Why are you a pirate?"

Husk lowered his instrument. "You ever go on board one of those ships we take?"

Aaron shook his head.

"Well, you ought to go and see what it's like. Drinking water all slimy . . . food goes bad, runs out . . . reduced to eating the vermin that took the last of it. Even when things ain't so bad it's no fun. Squat for pay, no stops in the ports. Why would I go back to that?"

"To do something that's . . ." He didn't want to say honest. Instead, he tried again. "Doesn't it bother you— what we're doing?"

"What are we doing that's so terrible?" Husk challenged. "Usually put the flag up and they're glad to give us all they got. You've seen it yourself, boy! Half the time they want to join us! We got the food, the drink, the good sailor's life's what we got. If you've got no family and love the sea . . . then this is the place to be!"

As if trying to convince Aaron, Husk touched his bow to the strings and launched into a bright and merry jig.

Maybe Husk was right. If it weren't for Pell, maybe he could get used to it . . . learn to love it as the others did.

Maybe.

But somehow Aaron didn't really think so.

As they had done before, the two ships prowled the seas together. Bonnet spent more and more time visiting Blackbeard aboard the *Queen Anne's Revenge*, and one day, Mullet ordered Aaron to take some provisions to Bonnet in Blackbeard's quarters.

"I think if you'll help me out . . . just for a brief time . . ." Bonnet was saying to Blackbeard as Aaron entered the room. The two men were sitting opposite each other, Blackbeard leaning back in the chair, his legs spread casually, a tankard of ale in his hand. Bonnet, on the other hand, sat straight up, as if a rod had been grafted to his spine.

"I helped you out before," Blackbeard replied, sounding almost bored.

"I was barely able to walk," Bonnet protested indignantly, puffing his chest out.

"You were well recovered by the time I left you."

Bonnet seemed flustered. He glanced up at Aaron, who stood awkwardly, carrying the box Mullet had sent him with. Bonnet gestured to a corner of the room and Aaron set the box down and headed toward the door.

"I think you're out of options," Blackbeard was saying as Aaron quietly left the room and shut the door behind him.

The rowboat that Aaron had tied below the *Queen Anne's Revenge* still had two more boxes that he had been ordered to deliver to Bonnet. As he reached the rail, Aaron swung a leg over and grabbed the ropes, preparing to climb down. That was when he heard footsteps behind him.

He knew it was Pell before he even turned and looked.

Pell had stopped just feet from him and stood staring at Aaron, not moving. Worried about how any movement on his own part might be construed, Aaron stared right back, trying not to even blink, but his blood turned to ice.

Pell was heavier than Aaron remembered, and his clothes were less ragged. His tan pants were free of any holes, and the leather vest he wore was faded, but not filthy or battle-scarred. This version of Pell looked slightly more prosperous and the glittering hate in his eyes more settled, more defiant.

What should he do? Aaron wondered, trying to unfreeze his brain. Scramble down the ropes to the rowboat? Yell loudly and hope that Husk was near? These choices seemed to give Pell so much power . . . power that Aaron decided he wasn't willing to give up so easily.

What if Aaron didn't care what Pell did to him? Then there would be no way left for Pell to hurt him.

Aaron stayed where he was, straddling the rail, and set his jaw, bracing himself for the unknown.

Pell's lips parted in a familiar, slow smile and he drew his hand up next to his face. Like a magician, Pell swiveled his wrist, opened his clenched fist, and revealed what was inside.

A single, bright red feather.

He had kept it. Actually *kept* it for all these months.

Why did it surprise Aaron so that Pell still managed to hurt him? He gripped the rail tightly, trying to keep an even expression on his face as Pell laughed softly and turned, striding slowly away.

Aaron stared after him for a long moment before lowering himself to the rowboat to retrieve the next box.

The following day, Blackbeard called the crew of the *Revenge* together. Pell stood on one side of Blackbeard while

Bonnet shifted uncomfortably on the other. Aaron came up behind the crew of pirates, stretching and straining his neck to keep the speaker in his sights.

"Your Major is too fine a gentleman to endure the rigors of running a ship," Blackbeard began, as Bonnet clasped his hands behind his back and avoided looking at the crowd.

"I have invited your captain to become a guest on board my ship," Blackbeard continued, "and I am pleased to tell you that he has accepted."

Bonnet rocked back and forth on his heels and looked down at his feet as Blackbeard continued.

"Do not worry, however, for you will not be without a captain. I am offering to you one of my own men to command your ship, and I am certain you will find him quite capable of running the *Revenge* in a satisfactory manner."

Not Pell, not Pell, Aaron pleaded mentally. *Just as long as it's not Pell.*

"I give you my own . . ." Aaron held his breath as Blackbeard finished. "Lieutenant Richards!"

The men began whooping and hollering and Bonnet looked at them, his quivering lips drawn and tight, as if he was fighting a sneer. Richards stepped forward and surveyed his new crew.

Aaron exhaled in relief.

At Turniff, *ten Leagues short of the Bay of* Honduras, *the Pyrates took in fresh Water; and while they were at an Anchor there, they saw a Sloop coming in, whereupon,* Richards *in the sloop called the* Revenge, *slipped his Cable, and run out to meet her; who upon seeing the black Flag hoisted, struck her Sail and came to, under the Stern of Teach the* Commadore. *She was called the* Adventure, *from* Jamaica, David Harriot *Master. They took him and his Men aboard the great Ship, and sent a Number of other Hands with* Israel Hands, *Master of* Teach's Ship, *to man the Sloop for the pyratical Account.*

—*Daniel Defoe*

~ ~ ~

The *Adventure*

After Lieutenant Richards was appointed as captain of the *Revenge*, he and Blackbeard formed a powerful team. The young captain, fierce, dashing, and as fiery as his red hair, was an enthusiastic cohort for Blackbeard. Bonnet, on the other hand, was pale, wan, and clearly brooding. Aaron saw him often, standing on the deck of the *Queen Anne's Revenge*, staring forlornly at his former ship.

Under Blackbeard's command, the two boats captured prize after prize. The cargo of the ships varied and the men never knew what they might find. Sometimes they would acquire gold and silver, although usually in small amounts. More often they found rum, sugar and molasses, indigo, ivory, or slaves. Sometimes the slaves were released back to the crew, but often they were presented with the chance to regain their freedom if they agreed to join the pirates, and a tremendous number took Blackbeard up on his offer. Employed men from the various captured ships often joined as well. Aaron assumed that—as Husk had explained to him months earlier—they were attracted to a life that appeared better than what they'd been enduring for months at sea. Whatever the reason, as the number of able-bodied workers on the boats swelled, each man's workload dwindled while their profits soared.

On a sultry July afternoon they came across a ship named the *Adventure* and Blackbeard decided not only to capture her, but to add her and her crew to his tiny fleet. The captain of the *Adventure*, David Harriot, a short man with beady, dark eyes, hardly needed any prodding to join with the pirates. A few men from his crew fought, and a few others tried to escape, but their bodies were quickly thrown from the *Adventure* into the undulating waves below. The remaining members of the crew quickly agreed that Harriot had the right idea, and they joined as well.

At the time, it seemed that this was just another in a long string of events that would barely have any effect on Aaron besides the remorse he felt over the murdered crewmen.

As it turned out, however, the decisions made that day were destined to change his life forever.

Blackbeard's quartermaster, Israel Hands, was appointed captain of the *Adventure* while Harriot joined Bonnet as a guest aboard the *Queen Anne's Revenge*. Shipmates were swopped as well. Some of the crew members from the *Adventure* joined the *Revenge*, some climbed aboard the *Queen Anne's Revenge*, and a few men from the *Revenge* switched over to the *Adventure*. Aaron stayed on the *Revenge* and was beyond dismayed to find that Pell and Vander were both reassigned there as well. Husk was one of the others assigned to the *Adventure*, and Aaron was sorry to see him go.

On their second evening together, as the three ships put down their anchors, Richards ordered Aaron to take a pot of salmagundi to Blackbeard's quarters. When he reached the cabin, Aaron found Harriot and Bonnet talking quietly and a boy, not much younger than himself, pouring rum for the two men. Blackbeard was nowhere in sight.

The boy took the pot from Aaron, lowering his eyes to the floor, and dished up the bowls of stew for Bonnet and Harriot. Aaron couldn't help but notice that the lad was slim, to the point of looking underfed, and his dark, shoulder-length hair that he wore tucked behind his ears was the straightest Aaron had ever seen.

Harriot speared a piece of meat and began chewing, but Bonnet only stared at his food.

"Jonathan," Harriot said through a full mouth, pointing to Bonnet's bowl, "it looks as if the Major is not hungry. You may as well take it away."

The boy reached for the stew, but Bonnet slapped his hand away and picked up a knife. The scowl on his chiseled face deepened as he, too, stabbed a piece of meat.

"Just eat his food," Harriot whispered conspiratorially to Bonnet. "Drink his rum. Let his men run your ship. And then, when they take a prize, let him give you your full share."

Aaron was looking at Jonathan, but the boy hadn't raised his eyes the entire time the men were talking.

"I want my ship back," Bonnet grumbled.

Harriot laughed and Bonnet scowled, glancing up at Aaron, but Aaron was barely paying attention to the men—Jonathan was the person closest to his own age that he had seen since leaving Barbados and Aaron desperately wanted to speak with him.

Having delivered the salmagundi, however, Aaron knew he couldn't stand around awkwardly any longer. He turned to leave, but as he did, he glanced back at Jonathan and made up his mind that he was going to find a way to talk with the boy soon.

As it turned out, he didn't have long to wait.

A few afternoons later when Aaron entered the hold of the *Revenge*—knife out and ready as always—he was startled to find Jonathan crouched in the corner with his back to Aaron. Suddenly realizing he was not alone, Jonathan scurried to his feet and spun on Aaron with a look of surprise.

"What are you doing?" Aaron asked, not sounding as friendly as he'd intended. Jonathan's eyes darted to Aaron's knife and his look of surprise turned to fear.

"N-nothing," Jonathan stammered. He dropped his head and tried to shoulder past Aaron. Aaron blocked his path.

"I'm not going to hurt you," Aaron said, struggling to put the knife away. "I just want to know what you're doing."

Before the boy had a chance to answer a voice from behind called out, "Jonathan?"

Aaron turned around and found himself face-to-face with yet another lad. He looked to be only a few years older than Aaron, although he was much taller than himself or Jonathan. Unlike Jonathan's dark, straight hair, this young man had light, curly hair, and even in the dim light of the hold, Aaron could tell that his startling direct, hazel eyes contrasted sharply to Jonathan's dark brown ones.

"I'm right here, Thomas!"

The hazel eyes shot past Aaron's shoulder to the younger boy. "What are you doing, Jonathan?"

"Nothing," Jonathan answered with a slightly guilty edge to his voice.

The newcomer looked back at Aaron questioningly and Aaron shrugged as if to say he had no idea what Jonathan was doing either.

"I'm Thomas Nichols," he said, shoving his hand toward Aaron. "This is my brother Jonathan."

"I'm Aaron Lee," Aaron replied, shaking the boy's hand.

"We'd better go," Thomas said, motioning to his brother, and before Aaron could reply, Jonathan slipped past him and the brothers disappeared up the ladder.

Strangely, Aaron immediately missed them both.

He wandered over to where Jonathan had been crouching and looked at the floor. One of the green sea turtles sat in the corner with a carrot lying in front of its face.

The sea turtles were kept in the hold as a supply of fresh meat, sometimes accompanied by pigs, chickens, or an occasional goat. They were quite large—Aaron often had to get someone to help him when it was time to take one to the galley. All the other turtles were as he had left them—placidly on their backs—but this turtle had been moved . . . and was flipped upright.

Aaron knelt down and examined the turtle. It had come to the hold with a chip the size of Aaron's fist missing from its back and a thin, partially healed crack across the width its shell. Aaron picked up the carrot and then rose to his feet. His eyes went to the burlap bag of carrots suspended from the ceiling. The bag was still tied securely, but the knot looked somehow different than the one he usually tied. Puzzled, he looked back at the turtle and shrugged at Jonathan's odd choice for sympathy.

Too bad; turtle soup was pretty tasty.

Not interested in spending any more time on compassion for his dinner, Aaron struggled to flip the turtle back over onto its back and then walked away.

Aboard the *Revenge*, Aaron saw Thomas at a distance several times over the next few days as the ships sailed together, but Jonathan stayed on Blackbeard's ship. Aaron found himself looking for them both often, somehow hoping he would have another opportunity to speak with them.

His chance came when he stumbled upon both Thomas and Jonathan, once again down in the hold. He stepped off the ladder, spotted the two boys crouching over something in the corner, and—determined to sound more friendly this time—said, "Oh. Hello."

Both Jonathan and Thomas rose quickly from where they were huddled, turning to face Aaron. Both boys looked vaguely guilty and shuffled their feet nervously.

"Hi," Thomas replied with a jerky wave, but Jonathan did not make a sound. Despite the companionship of his older brother, he seemed only slightly more comfortable than he had the last time they met.

"What are you doing here?" Aaron asked, hoping to sound casual.

"Jonathan likes this turtle," Thomas said, stepping aside to reveal the turtle with the damaged shell, flipped upright again. "He named her Mary."

"Oh, you mean Sal?" Aaron asked.

All of a sudden Jonathan found his voice. "You named her too?" he inquired eagerly, his dark eyes finally happy.

"Oh, yes, I call her Sal."

"Sal . . . ," Jonathan repeated.

"Yes, it's short for Salmagundi," Aaron explained, catching Thomas' eye and trying not to smile.

Thomas suppressed a laugh, but Jonathan gasped and moved protectively in front of the turtle, his eyes round as saucers. "Oh! Don't call her that!"

"He's just teasing you, Jonathan," Thomas explained.

"Oh," Jonathan said again, his shoulders dropping a little. "Well, it's not funny."

"No, it's not," Aaron said. "It's delicious!"

This time Thomas laughed out loud and Aaron smiled, but Jonathan used every muscle in his face to scowl at them. Aaron tried to reassure him, "I really am just kidding. We should definitely call her Mary."

Jonathan's bit his lip, then let some of the tension out of his brow.

"How do you know it's a she?" Aaron asked.

Jonathan dropped down beside the turtle and stroked her head. "Look at her," he said, raising his eyes to the two older boys, "she's much too pretty to be a boy."

Aaron cocked his head to one side and tried to look at the turtle objectively. He guessed she was pretty, as far as turtles went.

Jonathan turned back to Mary and tried to feed her a carrot while Aaron and Thomas struck up a friendly conversation.

Thomas told Aaron they had been working together for David Harriot on the *Adventure* for about eight months before the pirates took over. Once they had been captured, Thomas was reassigned to the *Revenge*, while Jonathan took on serving duties for Blackbeard, Harriot, and Bonnet on board the *Queen Anne's Revenge*.

As Thomas spoke of their duties, all three realized that they had work to do and acknowledged that they'd best get to it. Feeling a little lonely and a little lost when the brothers left again, Aaron shuffled over to Mary and squatted down next to her. She looked up at him and blinked. He smiled gently at her.

"I'm sorry," he said, reaching out to stroke her with one finger under her chin, "but you've got to go on your back again now."

Before he flipped her, however, Aaron regarded her quietly for a moment, then leaned in and whispered, "Jonathan's right, you know. You *are* kind of pretty."

Which now of these three, thinkest thou, was neighbor unto him
that fell among thieves?
—St. Luke 10:36

~ ~ ~

The Caymans

The ships, anchored off Grand Cayman, bobbed and rocked in a gentle breeze that smelled to Aaron of coconut and salt. They had captured eight ships over the last few weeks and most of the men had now gone ashore to celebrate their bounty. The *Revenge*'s captain, Lieutenant Richards, was on the *Queen Anne's Revenge*, visiting, and there was little work for Aaron to do. He stood at the rail, gazing toward the town surrounded by lush mountains, trying to decide whether to go ashore himself. Port Royal and Havana had certainly not been any fun, but he had been alone then . . . he hadn't known Thomas and Jonathan. Aaron considered asking them to visit the island with him, but something held him back.

Since their last meeting in the hold, he had seen Thomas on board every day and was often tempted to speak to him, but he never did. Aaron was worried that Pell would spot the two of them talking.

Aaron was certain if it was discovered that there was anything that brought Aaron even the smallest amount of happiness, Pell would try to destroy it. And so—though he feared Thomas might take offense—Aaron stayed below deck as much as possible and avoided Thomas' eyes whenever he was near. He was fiercely protecting something . . . he just wasn't sure exactly what.

Aaron had just made the final decision to stick with his gut instinct and not invite the brothers to accompany him to shore when he spotted Jonathan scaling the ropes on the side of the ship. He knew exactly where the boy was going even before he darted below deck. Every few days Aaron would find Mary flipped over with uneaten carrots lying beside her, and now he shook his head, smiling, as Jonathan disappeared from sight.

Just as Aaron was toying with the idea of visiting with Jonathan in the hold, he spotted Pell striding across the deck. He watched as Pell slipped down the hole and a sickening feeling engulfed him as he realized where Pell was going. And what he was going to do.

Aaron needed to find Thomas.

A desperate glance around the deck made it plain that Thomas was not above board. Aaron's eyes quickly searched the decks of the *Queen Anne's Revenge* and the *Adventure* as well but saw no sign of him there either. For all he knew, Thomas had gone to shore.

Heart racing, Aaron knew he couldn't wait any longer. He grabbed a lantern and raced to the hold.

He stopped just outside the entrance and peered in cautiously. Jonathan was backing away from Pell, his eyes wide with confusion and terror. Pell spoke so softly to the boy that Aaron couldn't make out the words, but the intent was as clear as a dog's growl.

He thought briefly of trying to find Thomas again, but there was no time. Aaron pulled the knife from his waist, thrust the lantern into the hold, and let his fury override his fear.

"Leave him alone."

Pell spun around, spied his very own knife in Aaron's hand, and laughed softly. His dark eyes glittered dangerously.

"*You* intend to stop me?"

Aaron nodded.

Pell grabbed Jonathan and wrapped an arm around his neck so swiftly that Aaron barely had time to blink. Pell snatched Jonathan up from the floor and held him fast. The boy's feet dangled above the floor as he struggled feebly, his hands clawing at his neck, trying to loosen Pell's hold.

Aaron stood, frozen.

"Do you want me to kill him?"

56

It would likely be better than the alternative, Aaron thought, but he shook his head.

"Then you'll set the knife down," Pell said.

Aaron hesitated and Pell wrenched Jonathan closer.

"I said set the knife down."

Aaron set the knife on the floor.

"Kick it to me," Pell said.

Aaron put his foot on the knife and slid it across the floor toward Pell. Pell dropped Jonathan to the floor and reached for his knife. Jonathan scrambled to his feet and retreated to the farthest corner.

"Get out of here, Jonathan," Aaron said quietly, surprising himself with the calm and steel in his voice. Not taking his eyes off Pell, he stepped to one side to give Jonathan plenty of room to escape, but Jonathan didn't move.

"You need to *leave*, Jonathan," Aaron insisted. He glanced away from Pell long enough to see that Jonathan was finally edging along the wall, slowly making his way toward the door.

"Well, one of you is staying," Pell said, drawing closer to them.

"Go on!" Aaron shouted to Jonathan. "Get out now!"

Aaron's shout shattered Jonathan's hesitancy, and the lad finally bolted for the door as Pell headed straight toward Aaron with the knife. Aaron had nowhere to go; if he moved away from Pell he would block Jonathan's escape.

Swinging the lantern forward with all his might to ward off the attack, he struck Pell in the arm.

The knife clattered to the floor and Aaron threw a punch with his free hand. His fist landed on the bridge of Pell's nose and Pell dropped to one knee, grabbing for the knife with one hand and his nose with the other. Aaron swiftly slammed his foot down on the knife just before Pell's hand reached it.

Aaron didn't know whether to try to grab the knife or to make an escape before Pell could get to his feet. He glanced behind him to make sure that Jonathan was safely gone but instead found him standing in the doorway, wide-eyed, chest heaving.

"Get out of here!" Aaron yelled at him, and Jonathan turned to leave. He bumped directly into Thomas, who had appeared suddenly in the doorway.

"What's going on?" Thomas asked in mild alarm, surveying the scene before him. He gently moved Jonathan aside, approached Aaron, and looked down at Pell. The pirate rose to his feet wearing a bone-chilling sneer, partially hidden by stringy hair, as Thomas turned toward Aaron.

"Is everything all right?"

Aaron expected a fight, but Pell backed up a step and surveyed the three boys. He was only slightly taller than Thomas, and Aaron could almost hear his thoughts: *It was three against one . . . they had youth on their side . . . his knife was under Aaron's foot.*

"Everything's fine," Pell said swaying just a bit. "Just fine."

He pushed his greasy, graying hair out of his face and then took a step toward Aaron.

"We'll finish our business later," he whispered, leaning in. Aaron felt the hot breath on his face and smelled the stench of rum.

Jonathan shrank behind Thomas as Pell swaggered out the doorway. Cautiously, Aaron leaned down to pick up the knife.

Thomas turned to Jonathan. "You've got to quit coming here," he told his younger brother tersely.

Aaron hurried over to the corner where the turtles were. As expected, Mary was upright again. Jonathan had gotten that far before Pell found him.

Aaron grabbed a bucket from a hook, dipped it in a barrel, and filled it with water.

"Harriot said I could," Jonathan said.

"Only because he's trying to be nice to you, Jonathan."

"I wanted to see Mary . . ."

58

"You *need* to stay on your ship."

Feeling like an interloper, Aaron flipped Mary back over and splashed the water from the bucket on her.

"But . . . but I miss you."

"I know you do, Jonathan. I miss you too. But it isn't safe for you to come here. Do you promise me you'll stay on your ship?"

Aaron filled another bucket. He didn't look up, but he heard the sniffling. It sounded like Jonathan was crying.

"I love you, Jonathan. I don't want anything to happen to you."

"When are we going to get out of here?" He was definitely crying now.

"I don't know," Thomas said, sounding weary. Their voices muffled, as if the brothers were hugging. "I just don't know."

Thomas looked over the top of his brother's head at Aaron. "You'll be all right?"

Aaron threw the second bucketful of water on the rest of the turtles, looked at Thomas, and then nodded.

"He'll leave you alone?"

No.

He wasn't going to be all right. Pell wasn't going to leave him alone. Aaron didn't know what Pell was going to do, but he knew it would be something terrible. Several possibilities were darting about in his mind and he felt his cheeks flush with shame.

"I'll be all right," he answered.

Thomas nodded as he put his arm around Jonathan's shoulder and guided him out the door.

After one step, though, Jonathan stopped and turned back to Aaron.

"Thank you . . ." he managed before beginning to cry again.

"You're welcome," Aaron said, his voice barely above a whisper. And then they were gone.

Pell retaliated before they even left the Caymans.

It was the next evening. Most of the crew was onshore, and Aaron had just finished filling a bucket from the huge tub of drinking water on deck. He turned and found himself gaping into Pell's wicked eyes. Pell bumped roughly into him, water sloshed over both of them, and Aaron dropped the bucket.

Grabbing Aaron's neck, Pell swiftly shoved him to the deck. In a smooth and lightning-quick movement, he stepped on Aaron's back, pinning his body to the wet wood as prickly slivers of the deck ground into Aaron's cheek and heart-pounding fear iced his veins. Pell dropped to the deck and ground one knee like a bone-crushing spike into Aaron's back and grabbed a handful of Aaron's thick, wavy hair, yanking his head back. White-hot stars of pain exploded behind Aaron's eyes and his breath came in short gasps as Pell whispered in his ear.

"You think you're something special?" he hissed. "You think you should be the only one?"

Aaron twisted and kicked as Pell lifted him by the hair.

"I hope it was worth it," Pell said, jerking Aaron to his feet and plunging his head deep beneath the surface of the tub. As the water enveloped him, so did a bottomless terror as Aaron realized that Pell was going to drown him. He struggled crazily, fighting against Pell's vice-like fingers entangled in his hair. Aaron flailed like a wild man, clawing at Pell's hands and writhing desperately, trying to lift his head out of the water. He scraped his fingers along the sides of the tub digging for a grip that would help him. He panicked as he inhaled his first breath of water. It scalded his lungs and burnt his throat, but then his body and mind relaxed, drifted, and a gray fog reached for him.

I hope it was worth it.

Aaron thought of Jonathan, walking safely out of the hold, and he actually smiled.

It had been worth it.

Aaron came to, coughing and vomiting on the wet deck of the ship. His chest hurt, as if someone had stood on him for days on end. Slivers of wood throbbed beneath his fingernails and he shivered uncontrollably. Half a dozen men surrounded him, most watching with bored distraction, and Aaron sat up, not comprehending what had happened. Suddenly he remembered and he looked around in fear, but Pell was nowhere to be seen.

He spotted Thomas in the small crowd of men and felt shame wash over him. Aaron scrambled to his feet. He fled to the darkness of the hold and sank to the floor. Wrapping his arms around his knees, Aaron gripped his knife tightly and stared in dazed fear at the door; hours later, his body finally stopped shivering enough for him to drag himself to bed on shaky legs.

That night Aaron dreamed that his mother hadn't died. *She was going to be upset because he'd been at sea and now her garden was overrun with weeds . . .*

He woke with a start and lay awake in his bed. Unable to fall back asleep, he went above deck and walked to the rail. Lopez and Mullet, standing guard, paid him no mind. The sea was exceptionally calm and reflected the full moon with shimmering brilliance. He stood for some time gazing at the night sky, dusted with diamonds, finding solace in the warm wind that gently caressed him.

What *would* his mother say if she could see him now? Aaron knew she wouldn't be upset about her garden, but she would be mortified that he was sailing around with a bunch of pirates.

She would want him to be safe.

Suddenly he heard footsteps and he reached for his knife before he spun around.

It was Thomas.

"Hello," Thomas said. His eyes fell on the knife. "Are you all right?"

Aaron fumbled to put the knife away. "I'm fine."

Thomas casually slid up to the rail beside him and they stood gazing at the bobbing, silhouetted *Queen Anne's Revenge* until Thomas broke the silence.

"I worry about him."

They glanced at each other and then back at the ship as Thomas went on. "I've been looking out for him ever since . . ."

His voice faded off.

"Our mother died when he was born," he finally finished.

Self-pity pulsed through Aaron's veins at the thought that no one had been looking out for him since *his* mother had died.

"Our dad passed away about three years ago," Thomas continued. "My uncle took us in after that, but somehow it feels like it's just me and Jonathan against the world—do you know what I mean?"

Aaron nodded, but he had no idea and he felt even sorrier for himself. He knew what it was like to be alone against the world, but not to have someone against it with him.

"We were to work with Harriot for about a year to assist my uncle," Thomas continued. "I promised I'd take care of Jonathan." He paused for a moment before adding, "I'm not doing a very good job." Guilt choked his voice.

Aaron didn't know what to say, so he kept quiet and waited for Thomas to keep talking.

"Harriot was really good to us—especially to Jonathan. Jonathan liked him a lot. I didn't think he was the kind of man who would have joined Blackbeard. Somehow I was counting on him to do the right thing, but I guess that's not going to happen."

"Have you thought about trying to escape?" Aaron asked.

Thomas grew quiet for a moment before responding and Aaron thought he heard the softest sigh. "When they first took over, my friend Jonas tried to escape."

"What happened?"

Thomas didn't answer, but Aaron remembered the bodies being thrown from the *Adventure*.

"I'm sorry," Aaron said quietly.

They settled into another period of silence.

"How did you get here?" Thomas finally asked.

"My mother died," Aaron said, as if that somehow explained everything.

"Oh," Thomas said softly. "What about your father?"

This time it was Aaron's turn not to answer.

"Oh," Thomas said again, and Aaron knew he had taken this to mean that his father was dead too.

Aaron didn't correct him.

A faithful friend is a sturdy shelter: he that has found one has found a treasure. There is nothing so precious as a faithful friend, and no scales can measure his excellence. A faithful friend is an elixir of life; and those who fear the Lord will find him.
—Sirach 6:14–16

~ ~ ~

Nassau

If Aaron weren't so alone, he knew he wouldn't be such an easy target for Pell, yet he couldn't bring himself to jeopardize the fledgling friendship with Thomas and Jonathan that had begun to form. He was still afraid that if Pell sensed any semblance of camaraderie between the boys he would do whatever he could to destroy it—as he had Rosalie.

Over the next few weeks, Aaron took every opportunity to visit the *Queen Anne's Revenge*, and—while he was there—he would always check on Jonathan. Upon his return from Blackbeard's ship, Aaron made certain Thomas knew that Jonathan was all right by simply catching his eye and giving him the slightest of nods and the briefest of smiles. Thomas somehow seemed to understand the importance of not being seen together and he would discreetly return a slight nod and brief smile as well.

He understood. *Everything was all right.*

Meanwhile, Blackbeard captured a Spanish sloop, named it the *Caesar*, and added it to his fleet. The legendary pirate was now in command of four ships that easily defeated any prey they encountered, and by the time the pirates sailed once again to the Bahamas and dropped anchor in Nassau's harbor, their pockets were full of gold.

Only after most of the men—including Pell—were ashore, did Aaron venture to the rail and stare at the island. She was lush and green, edged with jagged, mysterious mountains, and her bay brimmed with white-sailed ships.

Her docks thronged with hoards of people bustling about with great speed and deliberation. It seemed no one wasted much time in Nassau. Debating what to do with himself, he rested his chin on his hands.

"Would you like to come with us?"

Aaron turned around to meet Thomas' hopeful gaze.

"Jonathan and I are going ashore," Thomas explained. "Do you want to go?"

Surely they could avoid Pell in such a crowded place . . .

"Yes!" Aaron nodded, feeling suddenly reckless and holding back a foolish grin.

Once in town the three bobbed and weaved through the masses and explored the waterfront before finally deciding to have lunch in a small tavern.

As they stepped inside the dark, noisy establishment, Aaron said, "It's going to feel good to eat something I didn't have to make myself."

"I'm certain it's going to *taste* a lot better too," Thomas said, and Jonathan laughed.

"You're quite clever," Aaron smirked, but as he slid into a squeaking, wobbly chair he realized that this would be the first meal he hadn't cooked for himself since his mother had died. He chased this sad thought from his mind, determined to have a good time on the island.

"Well," he looked at Jonathan as the brothers sat down, "I wonder if they have salmagundi?"

"You're quite clever too," Jonathan said, trying unsuccessfully to suppress a smile. "How is Mary, anyway? I haven't seen her in so many days."

"She's fine," Aaron said. "One of the ships they took last week was a turtler, so it'll be a while before I have to use her."

Jonathan frowned at the mention of the fact that one day Aaron would likely have no choice other than to feed Mary to the pirates.

"Can we not let her go?" Jonathan asked sounding heartbroken over the turtle's destiny. "Just set her free so she'll be happy?"

"I'm having a difficult enough time aboard that ship without getting caught throwing food overboard," Aaron said, hoping he didn't sound too melodramatic. "Besides, I kind of like having her around." There were times when a brief visit to Mary was the only good thing that would happen to him in an entire day.

"I know," Jonathan sighed. "I just don't want anything to happen to her."

"I don't either," Aaron assured him, "but as I said, I don't think it's going to be a problem for a few months."

"If it looks as if you'll be needing her," Thomas said, "you can let me know and maybe we can take a chance on releasing her. Until then, I think we should just leave things the way they are."

"You're right," Jonathan agreed. "That's what we should do."

Aaron smiled to himself. It felt awfully good to be included in a discussion about what *we* should do.

A few days later, the three friends strolled casually on a snow-white beach just outside of town. Thomas suddenly flashed his brother a huge grin and started snatching at the buttons on his shirt.

"What are you doing?" Jonathan asked.

Grinning, Thomas tossed the shirt over his shoulder and jerked his thumb at the water. "I'm going swimming!"

Jonathan and Aaron smiled and started undressing too. Aaron had just lifted his shirt over his head when he heard Jonathan gasp and Thomas curse—something Aaron had not heard him do before. He removed his shirt quickly, trying to imagine what had happened.

They were looking at him. At his throat and chest. At his scar.

"What happened to you?" Thomas asked in a low voice.

"Nothing," Aaron said angrily, struggling to put his shirt back on.

66

"Don't," Thomas said, putting out a restraining hand. "I'm sorry. I shouldn't have said anything. Please swim with us."

"No," Aaron said, readying to pull his shirt over his head. "I don't want to."

"Don't be angry. Please come with us."

"Please?" Jonathan begged.

Aaron studied the hurt looks on their faces.

"We'll pretend we never saw a thing," Thomas added. "Right, Jonathan?"

"Saw what?" Jonathan deadpanned.

The two looked at Aaron expectantly and he looked back, pondering their hopeful eyes. The hazel of Thomas' eyes was so much lighter than the dark brown of Jonathan's, but they were exactly the same in shape, and Aaron was almost jealous of their brotherly bond. He looked back and forth between the two and realized they were offering at least a taste of that bond.

He sighed, then nodded, and that was all Thomas and Jonathan needed. They turned and raced down to the surf and Aaron walked slowly behind, taking his shirt back off as he followed and wondering if he would ever be able to enjoy anything again without being haunted by his past.

Slade's tavern quickly became a favorite hangout of the pirates, and one day the three boys, feeling rather grown up, decided to try it. Aaron led them in the door, immediately spotted Pell at a front table, and backed up into Jonathan as panic iced his veins.

"I don't want to eat here," Aaron said, almost knocking Jonathan down.

"Why not?" he asked, obligingly backing up . . . not that he had any choice: Aaron was about to plow over him.

"I just don't want to," Aaron said, looking anywhere but at his friends.

Thomas peered into the doorway and then turned back to Aaron.

"He's not going to do anything to you," Thomas said in a quiet voice.

Before he could stop the words, Aaron gushed, "You don't have any idea what he's capable of," and he dropped his gaze to the ground.

"I know more than you think I do," Thomas said gently, putting his hand on Aaron's shoulder. "Trust me, all right? Nothing's going to happen."

Aaron wanted nothing more at that moment than to trust Thomas, but he shook his head. "No."

"Come on, Aaron," Jonathan said, tugging on Aaron's sleeve. "It'll be all right."

"No," Thomas said, looking more sympathetic. "We can go somewhere else."

Relief running deep, Aaron gratefully led them to another tavern, but his reprieve was short-lived as Thomas kept insisting that they try Slade's. Each day he would stick his head in the door and see which pirates were there (in what quickly became apparent were their usual spots) and then the three friends would go someplace else.

They arrived earlier and earlier each day, and on his fourth attempt, Thomas stuck his head in the door and announced that the tavern was all but empty. Aaron still did not want to go in, but this time, Thomas would not be swayed.

"Come on," he said. "There's hardly anyone in there— it's too early for them."

"What if they come in while we're there?" Aaron asked, well aware that he sounded like a scared child.

"We'll sit in the back—they'll never even see us."

Something in Thomas' eyes told Aaron that his mind was made up and, reluctantly, he allowed Thomas to lead him through the door.

They had barely taken their seats when Thomas rapped his knuckles on the table and announced he would be right back. Abruptly, he excused himself and headed toward the bar.

Scratching his head at Thomas' odd behavior, Aaron leaned toward Jonathan. "Why does he want to come in here so badly?"

"I don't know," Jonathan admitted, tucking a strand of straight, dark hair behind his ear.

Aaron drummed his fingers on the table and tried not to feel any resentment, but it bothered him that Thomas had been so persistent. Why would he insist on eating here when it clearly bothered Aaron so? There were plenty of other places to eat in Nassau.

As Aaron absently studied the carvings on the tavern table, he reminded himself that Thomas had been nothing but kind and obliging to him since the day they'd met.

If this is important to Thomas, Aaron decided, *the least I can do is not give him a hard time about it.*

Thomas returned and sat down. Jonathan looked at him and wrinkled his nose.

"What's that smell?" Jonathan asked.

Aaron smelled it too. It smelled like the pitch they used to repair ships.

"I wonder what's good to eat here?" Thomas said, blatantly ignoring Jonathan. Aaron and Jonathan shot each other questioning looks of which Thomas seemed to be completely oblivious.

By the time they finished eating their mouth-watering baked chicken seasoned with some exotic pepper, the large room had filled with laughing, beer-swilling pirates. Aaron stood to leave, but Thomas yanked his arm and tried to pull him back down.

"I think we should wait a while," Thomas said.

"Why?" Aaron asked, pulling his arm away.

Thomas nodded toward the door. Aaron's heart fluttered for a moment at the sight of Pell, but he composed himself and dropped quickly back into his seat.

"It's all right," he told Thomas. "We can go."

"No," Thomas said. "I think we should wait."

"Why?"

But Thomas wouldn't answer.

They waited for over an hour. Several times Aaron assured Thomas that he was perfectly capable of walking past Pell to leave, but Thomas remained emphatic that they stay.

With nothing to do but watch drunk pirates, Aaron and Jonathan grew bored. Just as Aaron was about to *insist* that they leave, Thomas nudged him and nodded in Pell's direction.

Aaron turned around. Pell had obviously tried to stand up from the table, but his stool had gone with him. It was firmly stuck to the seat of his pants. Brow deeply furrowed, he tried to pull it off, but it would not budge. He swung around like a dog after his own tail and the stool hit the table and upset it, clattering drinks and food to the floor amidst the roar of laughing men.

Befuddled, Aaron turned back around to find Thomas with his head on the table and his shoulders violently shaking with laughter.

"What did you do?" Aaron asked breathlessly.

Thomas lifted his head to answer, but he was laughing too hard to speak.

Jonathan's mouth dropped open and then he said, "I *knew* I smelled something!"

That made Thomas laugh harder. Aaron whirled around in time to see Vander prying the stool from Pell's backside, nearly ripping his breeches off in the process. Onlookers hooted, rolled, and guffawed like donkeys, slamming their mugs down on the tables and slapping their thighs.

Cursing his displeasure at being the butt of the joke, Pell demanded to see the owner. A tall, well-muscled negro wearing a bright red bandana and gold earring calmly walked around the bar and met the complaining pirate face-to-face. Pell let loose a string of obscenities and accusations on him that should have shocked even a pirate innkeeper. First looking confused and then throwing his head back to laugh, the man refused to take responsibility for the prank. Pell stormed from the restaurant with Vander at his heels.

The laughter died down shortly in the tavern, except at the back table, where it went on for some time.

During their last full day on the island, Aaron wiggled his toes in the warm sand and voiced what they were all feeling.

"I don't want to go back," he said with a heavy sigh.

The two brothers nodded in somber agreement, but then suddenly Jonathan's eyes brightened.

"Let's *not* go back!" he said. "Let's leave!"

"And where exactly do you propose we go?" Thomas asked.

"I don't know," Jonathan mumbled, chucking a seashell into the waves.

"We *can't* leave, Jonathan," Thomas said. He spoke slowly, enunciating every word to make sure his brother understood. "We're on an island. If we leave, they will *find* us and they will *kill* us."

"I know," Jonathan nodded. "Besides, we've got to think about Mary."

"Yes," Aaron said. "*That's* why I'm getting back on the pirate ship. Because of Mary."

They all laughed lightly before Thomas became serious again. He put a hand on Jonathan's arm.

"If I ever think we have a safe shot at escaping, we'll cut and run, but I'm not going to take a chance with our lives until then, all right?"

Jonathan nodded and Thomas looked at Aaron.

If you ever leave, Aaron thought, *I won't be able to go with you.*

He said nothing, however, and managed to give Thomas a nod. He filtered sand through his fingers over and over and thought about the day he would have to explain why he wouldn't leave with them—why he would instead stay with the pirates.

That will be the hardest thing I ever have to do, he thought dolefully. *That will be the day that you stop being my friends.*

71

~ ~ ~

The Bell

Aaron sat up with sand and broken bits of shells sticking to his back, his skin warm and salty.

How long had he been sleeping?

After the small fleet of ships had left Nassau, the pirates had cruised to some of the smaller islands in the Bahamas. They spent several leisurely days there, picking through the remains of shipwrecks and diving for bullion.

Before falling asleep, Aaron had been walking the beach with Thomas and Jonathan and they had all stopped to rest for a few minutes. He lay down on the warm, inviting sand and closed his eyes for just a moment, and the next thing he knew he was sitting up, wide awake, and Thomas and Jonathan were nowhere in sight.

Aaron hadn't felt so content since leaving Barbados. His entire body was warm—not just from the sun that was beating down on him but from something inside too. He grinned, remembering the look on Pell's face when he'd turned the table over. In a light mood, Aaron stood up to search for Thomas and Jonathan. He trotted down the beach, rounded a bend, and spotted Bonnet, a hundred yards or so out, picking through some wreckage the low tide had revealed. Bonnet beckoned to him, but Aaron pretended not to see and hurried the opposite way.

He walked a long time before he finally met Thomas and Jonathan coming toward him. He couldn't help but notice how shabby the brothers looked, silhouetted against the white beach. He wondered if his own clothes were as worn and his breeches as short as theirs. They were going to have to make time to outfit themselves and, judging by Thomas' wavy, light hair hanging in his eyes, haircuts were in order, too.

As they neared, Aaron realized that Thomas was carrying a large, brass bell.

"Let's hear it!" Aaron exclaimed once they were standing next to each other on the warm sand. Thomas swung the bell in a high arch, and a loud, crisp ring echoed through the air.

"May I try?" Aaron asked.

Thomas handed the bell to Aaron.

It was heavier than he expected and he had to practice a bit to get a good, resounding ring from it the way Thomas had. As he handed the bell back, an idea struck him and he asked them, "Do you want to play a game?"

They did.

It was a simple game—based loosely on the rules to one he had played in Barbados—and they chased each other around the beach for over an hour. Running from the gentle surf and into the thick brush at the edge of the sand, all three seemed to forget—if only for a little while—that four pirate ships were anchored offshore not far down the island. Every so often one of them made a mad dash for the bell, trying to ring it before getting tagged by the others.

After the boys tired of playing, they splashed in the surf to cool off and then lay back in the sun to warm up. Aaron was on the verge of falling asleep again when something light landed on his stomach. He brushed it off and didn't think much about it—until it happened again. He sat up on his elbows and looked at his stomach. There was a little shell on it. He looked over at Thomas and Jonathan who were grinning, each poised to lob another shell.

Aaron picked up the shell and threw it back at them.

"What are you so tired for?" Thomas asked. "You're not going to take another nap, are you?"

Aaron rolled over onto his stomach, shaking his head and smiling. How could he ever explain to them how relaxed he finally felt?

Still smiling, Aaron crossed his arms in front of him and put his head down on them. He closed his eyes again and took a deep breath, but Thomas and Jonathan had no intention of letting him rest any longer. A continual pelt of shells kept him from getting any more sleep that afternoon.

After the Bahamas, Blackbeard's fleet cruised to the coast of North Carolina and sailed up the Chowan River, stopping to careen at Holiday Island. Unlike the Bahamas, there was nothing to do here—no beach, no taverns, no shipwrecks, no surf. The surrounding land was overgrown and swampy, the water dark and mysteriously still. Buzzards circled just upstream. On the ocean, the wind had been constant company, pressing the heat away, but here, the air hung over them like a heavy weight, smothering their strength.

Lying on the deck of the *Revenge*, lazy and hot, Jonathan and Aaron stared up at a blue sky dotted with white, fluffy clouds. "Where's Thomas?"

"He wanted to be alone for a little while," Jonathan answered.

"Why?" Aaron asked, secretly fearing the reason. "Is he trying to figure out how to escape?"

"Oh, no," Jonathan replied in a low voice, "not here. He said we aren't going to try to get away until we're on the mainland and in a place where there are a lot of people— like Charles-Town or Savannah . . . someplace like that. It needs to be crowded enough so that we can just disappear . . ."

"This is on the mainland," Aaron said, pointing to the shore.

"I know, but Thomas says we'd wander around for days and probably starve to death because it's so desolate."

"Oh," Aaron said, relieved that the two weren't going to try to escape for at least a while.

"Don't worry," Jonathan continued. "He'll know when it's the right time."

I'm not worried, Aaron thought. *At least not about that.*

"So then why does he want to be alone?" Aaron asked, hoping to change the subject.

"I think he's trying to figure out what he's supposed to do."

"But it sounds like he's already got everything figured out . . ."

"No," Jonathan said, shaking his head. "Not about escaping."

"What then?"

Jonathan hesitated.

"What?" Aaron insisted, rolling over on his stomach and propping himself up on an elbow.

"Do you believe in God?" Jonathan finally asked, his voice even lower than when they had been discussing an escape.

Aaron nodded and Jonathan looked relieved.

"Well, I think he's trying to understand what God wants him to do."

"About what?"

"About being here with all these men who are so . . . so different from what we're used to."

"What do you mean?"

"He doesn't want us to become like them."

Aaron laughed softly. "I don't think he needs to worry about that."

"But it's easy to change if you're not careful," Jonathan said, his dark eyes pinning Aaron with a warning. "He's already doing things that he never would have done before . . ."

"Like what?"

"Like being deceitful . . ."

"When?" Aaron challenged doubtfully. "When has Thomas ever been deceitful?"

"All the time. He pretends that he's not planning on escaping, he acts as though he doesn't mind being here. When he sees somebody doing something wrong he doesn't try to stop them . . . he doesn't even say anything to them. That's deceitful."

"But if he doesn't act like that he'll get killed," Aaron said, not seeing the issue at all.

Jonathan nodded. "I know, but that's not how we were raised and he's just having a hard time."

Aaron shook his head and rolled back over on his back, making a pillow out of arms. "Well, I don't think he needs to feel bad at all . . . he's doing the best he can under the circumstances. I guess if you really want to look at it that way it *is* deceitful, but I don't think he has any choice."

"Maybe not," Jonathan agreed, "but he's doing other things too . . . things he *does* have a choice about."

"What?" Aaron asked, not able to imagine what Jonathan could be talking about.

"Like that prank he played on Pell in the tavern. That wasn't the right thing to do."

"Oh," Aaron said, sitting up with a smile, "that was wonderful! He doesn't need to feel bad about that. That was one of the funniest things I've ever seen in my life!"

"But it was mean," Jonathan argued. "He shouldn't have done it."

"You were laughing too," Aaron said. "Don't pretend it wasn't funny."

"It *was* funny," Jonathan admitted, a slight smile crossing his lips, "but it still wasn't the right thing to do."

Aaron lay back on his elbows again and shook his head. "I disagree," he said firmly, staring up at the mast with its mainsail lowered. "It was a brilliant thing to do. Pell deserves far worse than that."

"Well, Thomas feels bad about it now."

"He's wasting his efforts worrying," Aaron said, shooting back his own firm gaze.

"Here he comes," Jonathan said, looking past him. Aaron turned to see Thomas coming up from the hold.

76

"Please don't tell him what we've been talking about," Jonathan whispered, and Aaron nodded in agreement as the boys sat up.

"What are you two talking about?" Thomas asked as he approached them.

"Just trying to figure out why Blackbeard brought everyone up here to careen," Aaron said.

"The ships are in need of repair, I imagine," Thomas said, sitting cross-legged beside them.

"They aren't in *that* much need of it," Aaron argued, slapping a black fly off his arm. "Have you seen them? They're in good shape. We don't need to be here at all."

Jonathan shook his head. "I don't think we're here just to careen."

"Why not?"

"I heard Blackbeard and Hands talking," he explained in a low voice. "They're going somewhere."

"Going somewhere?" Aaron and Thomas chimed together.

"Yes. With Richards. They were going somewhere today."

Thomas frowned. "When?"

"I think they left before first light."

Aaron realized that Jonathan was right. He hadn't seen Richards all day. Where could the captains from three of their four ships possibly go in an area as desolate as this?

"Where did they go?" he asked out loud.

"Roy-hot-skue . . . Ar-hu-sky . . . I don't know."

"What?" Thomas laughed.

"I don't know what it's called," Jonathan said, tracking a mosquito that was intent on attacking one of them.

"Obviously," Aaron agreed, smacking the mosquito between his hands. The bugs in this place were worse than anything Aaron had ever seen.

"Some Indian name I think," Jonathan offered weakly. "They never said it the same way twice—I don't think they even know what it's called. Once it sounded like 'A-hot-sky'."

"Where is this 'Hot-sky'?" Thomas asked.

"I have no idea," Jonathan said.

Aaron stared up at the blue span above them. "I think 'A-hot-sky' is right here," he said, wiping his brow.

"Why did they want to go to 'A-hot-sky'?" Thomas pressed further.

"I have no idea," Jonathan repeated.

"You're a real plethora of information. You know that, don't you?" Thomas teased.

"I'm ready to go to 'A-cool-river'!" Aaron said, standing up. He swung a leg over the rail and looked back to see if Jonathan and Thomas were following him. They were, and he managed to jump just before he was pushed.

He hit the water hard, released his breath, and let himself sink into the depths of the river until his feet touched the cool mud on the bottom. He looked up at the surface, watching the sun scatter and waver as it cut through the water. Then Thomas and Jonathan plunged into the river with an explosion of bubbles, and Aaron kicked back toward the surface to join them.

When Blackbeard, Richards, and Hands returned near dusk, the boys were no closer to finding out where the three men had been than they were earlier in the afternoon. Each captain was filthy; they all tore their shirts off and jumped into the river almost immediately after they reached the ships. Blackbeard hollered for some rum, and Jonathan and Aaron fetched it immediately, tossing three bottles down from the railing to the laughing men in the river. Israel Hands sank under the water, holding only his bottle above the surface. He reappeared, took a large swig, and turned to face Richards. Aaron sucked in his breath when he saw Hands' back. It was so red with sunburn that Aaron wondered how he could bear it. Even from this distance, he could see blisters stretching the skin. Aaron nudged Jonathan, and they both watched as Richards turned his back to them and revealed skin just as badly burned.

"What on earth did they do to get so sunburned?" Aaron whispered to Jonathan.

"I don't know . . . is he sunburned too?" Jonathan nodded his head in Blackbeard's direction.

Both boys stared at Blackbeard for a moment, but his back and chest were so covered with black, curly hair that if the sun *had* been able to penetrate it, it was impossible to tell now. He was swimming without his hat, though, and the boys could see a hint of red on his nose.

They looked back to Hands and Richards, who were splashing each other like children playing in a tidal pool.

"They're going to be miserable," Jonathan said, and Aaron nodded in agreement.

"We may as well go fetch some more rum," Aaron said. "They're probably going to want to keep drinking."

Late that night a commotion woke Aaron from a deep sleep. Concerned, he raced up on deck where, beneath a full, glowing moon, he could see the deck of the *Queen Anne's Revenge*. At least a dozen men from the *Revenge* had gone over there, where someone was yelling and cursing at the top of his lungs.

In the silvery shadows of the other ship, Aaron could make out Thomas moving about the deck. Aaron went to the rail, straining to see Jonathan too, but he couldn't find him anywhere.

Worried, Aaron waited and waited until eventually Thomas glanced toward the *Revenge* and saw him. He paused and gave Aaron the slightest of nods and the briefest of smiles.

Everything was all right.

"What happened?" Aaron asked when Thomas finally returned to the *Revenge*.

"Blackbeard shot Hands," Thomas said as he took a seat on a keg of rum.

"*Why?*"

"I don't know," Thomas answered with a shrug. "Jonathan was actually there when it happened, but he didn't seem to want to talk much about it. All he would tell me is that Blackbeard pulled out a pistol under the table and shot Hands."

"Where did he get hit?" Aaron asked.

"In the knee."

Aaron winced. "Is he going to be all right?"

"He'll live," Thomas said. "But I don't think he'll ever walk properly again."

As they returned below deck, Hands' cries could still be heard echoing across the riverbanks.

. . . they plundered those vessels going home to England *from hence of about fifteen hundred Pounds Sterling, in Gold and Pieces of Eight. And after that, they had the most unheard-of Impudence to send up one* Richards, *and two or three more of the Pirates, with the said* Mr. Marks, *with a Message to the Government, to demand a Chest of Medicines of the Value of three or four hundred Pounds.*
—*Richard Allein, 1718*

~ ~ ~

Hostages

The ships headed downstream as soon as day broke and by afternoon they'd reached the ocean. Thomas found Aaron sitting atop a pile of rope at the stern, half-heartedly pushing a piece of tack around in some watery gravy. With too much excitement, Thomas reported that they were headed toward Charles-Town.

"Why are we going there?" Aaron asked, hoping he didn't sound as panicked as he felt. He thought about what Jonathan had told him regarding escape plans, and a great sadness settled over him.

"I'm not certain, but with the currents and the winds, I'd estimate we're traveling at about 30 knots. I expect we'll be there by tomorrow afternoon," Thomas predicted happily.

"How do you know that?"

"I navigated for Harriot," Thomas explained, apparently surprised at Aaron's question.

"Pardon?"

"On the *Adventure* . . . that's what I did for Harriot. I was his navigator."

"Oh," Aaron said, ashamed that he had never bothered to find this out before. "You must be really intelligent. You have to be intelligent to navigate."

Thomas smiled and sat down next to Aaron. "Well, then I must take after my father."

"Your father was a navigator?"

"No," he said, "my father was intelligent."

"What did your father do?" Aaron asked.

"He was a shipbuilder."

"Oh."

"What about your father?" Thomas asked.

"He, um . . ." Aaron shook his head and swallowed. Thomas seemed to sense his discomfort.

"If he was anything like you then I expect he was intelligent too," Thomas said quietly, clapping a hand on Aaron's shoulder and looking into his eyes with such great kindness that Aaron suddenly felt an overwhelming desire to tell him the truth.

"I'm nothing like my father," he managed to say.

"Oh?" Thomas tilted his head, inviting Aaron to go on.

But Aaron found the words were caught in his throat and he knew he wasn't going to be able to say anything else. He just shook his head at Thomas.

Thomas squeezed his shoulder. "Everything's going to be all right," he whispered. Aaron nodded and managed a weak smile before Thomas strode away, leaving him alone with his sadness.

Aaron threw his hardtack into the water and retreated below deck. The summer's heat seemed to be trapped directly above his bunk. He lay down and closed his eyes. Despite the heat and the fact that tomorrow he was going to lose the only two friends that he had in the world, Aaron couldn't stay awake for another moment. Exhausted, he drifted into a deep and dreamless sleep and didn't awaken until morning. When he awoke, he sequestered himself in the galley, mindlessly performing tasks.

And as Thomas predicted, they arrived off the coast of Charles-Town by afternoon.

Aaron took his time getting above deck. By the time he emerged, many men were straining to catch a glimpse of Charles-Town. The *Queen Anne's Revenge*, in the lead, dropped anchor at the entrance to the harbor, and Blackbeard shouted orders for the other ships to do the same.

"Why?" Thomas wondered aloud. "Why are we stopping here?"

A small ship sailed toward them from the port. It approached the *Queen Anne's Revenge* and was immediately seized by her crew.

"That was the pilot boat!" Thomas exclaimed. "They were supposed to follow her safely into the harbor!"

A square-rigged, three-masted boat followed, and Blackbeard took her over as well.

"What's he *doing?*" Thomas asked under his breath. Aaron saw the hope draining from his friend's eyes. Thomas slammed his fist down on the rail. "What does he think he's doing?" Aaron didn't answer.

Darkness fell. That night, Aaron lay awake, thinking of how quickly Thomas and Jonathan's chance at escape had dissipated like a morning fog. They couldn't go into Charles-Town now . . . every one of them would be wanted men. Whatever happened, they would have to leave without going into port, and that meant that Jonathan and Thomas wouldn't be able to escape.

And to his horror, Aaron realized that this thought made him happy.

I'm a terrible, truly terrible person. I think of them as my friends, and yet I'm glad they can't escape?

You're all alone and you're scared, he answered himself. *You can't help it. It's natural for you to want your friends to be with you, but if you had the chance to help them escape, you would.*

"I hope so," he whispered to himself, but he wondered. Would he? Would he really help them escape, or would he sabotage their efforts in order to keep them with him? He didn't want to believe that about himself, yet he couldn't deny how pleased he was that they wouldn't be visiting Charles-Town. He reached for a blanket and, despite the heat, pulled it around his shoulders and closed his eyes. Unlike the night before, sleep was a long time coming.

The following morning, the small flotilla began capturing more ships at the entrance to the Charles-Town harbor. By the end of the day, they had captured another eight and on the third day, Blackbeard called for Lieutenant Richards. Thomas quickly volunteered to row the captain over to the *Queen Anne's Revenge*. It was near nightfall by the time he returned, alone.

"Is Jonathan all right?" Aaron asked, turning from a pile of dirty dishes.

Thomas nodded.

"What did Blackbeard want Richards for?"

"He sent him and a few others to shore with one of the hostages," Thomas answered.

"Why?"

"He's demanding a ransom in exchange for the safe return of the boats and all their passengers."

"A ransom . . ." Aaron repeated slowly, the word sticking on his tongue like rotted meat.

"Hopefully," Thomas said, "if he gets what he wants, we'll leave and everything will get back to normal."

Aaron couldn't help but smile. "A few days ago you were planning to escape from 'normal', but now you're hoping to get back to it?"

Thomas nodded and smiled back. "I guess no matter how bad you think things are, they can always get worse."

If you only knew . . .

Within a few days, Aaron saw a small boat heading toward the *Queen Anne's Revenge*. Lieutenant Richards and a few other men were on board. They called for ropes to hoist a trunk aboard Blackbeard's ship. The captive ships were looted and the passengers, though relieved of everything but the clothes on their backs, were released unharmed. Blackbeard pulled up anchor and sailed north. The smaller ships stayed behind briefly, giving Blackbeard in his slow, massive ship a good head start, but then quickly caught up.

"I can't imagine what was in that chest," Thomas said aloud as the boys gathered at the rail to watch the small skiff sail back to port. "The Royal Navy is going to be after us. I hope it was worth it."

"The Royal Navy has always been after us," Aaron said blandly, turning his gaze from the town they'd just robbed to the open sea.

"But they'll be after us as never before now. The government isn't going to let him terrorize a town like that. He must realize that with *four* ships . . . one of them so big and slow . . ."

Thomas didn't finish his sentence. He was silent for a long time, unnerving Aaron.

"I think we're going to need to be more willing to take chances than we were before," he finally said. "Maybe we should have tried to escape when we were at 'A-hot-sky'." He lifted his eyes to Aaron. "If something happens to Jonathan I'll never forgive myself."

"Nothing's going to happen to Jonathan," Aaron said, "or you, or me. Everything's going to be fine. You'll escape . . . I'll help you." As he said the words he knew that he meant them and he felt immensely better about himself.

"Of course you'll help," Thomas said. "You're coming too."

"Oh," Aaron stammered. "I meant, I'll help you figure something out. I'm intelligent too, remember?"

Thomas laughed and slapped his friend on the back. "Thank you, Aaron."

Aaron smiled back and they watched as the South Carolina shoreline slipped from their view.

'Twas generally believed the said Thatch run his Vessel a-ground
on purpose to break up the Companies, and to secure what Moneys
and Effects he got for himself . . .
—David Harriot, 1718

~ ~ ~

Lightening the Load

Soon they arrived off the featureless, emerald-green coast of North Carolina. Blackbeard's ship was in the lead and—when she headed into an inlet—she stopped abruptly. Aaron watched in surprise as the monstrous ship suddenly began listing to one side.

Thomas appeared at Aaron's side.

"What's happening?" Aaron asked, alarmed.

But before Thomas could venture an answer, Lieutenant Richards, from his perch on the captain's deck, barked out, "She's on a sandbar!"

The other three ships in Blackbeard's posse hung back, their captains clearly uncertain what to do. All eyes were focused on the *Queen Anne's Revenge*, especially Aaron's and Thomas' as they searched anxiously for any sign of Jonathan.

Several minutes later a small boat left the stranded ship and headed toward the *Adventure*. She trailed behind her thick ropes, attached to the *Queen Anne's Revenge*, that were handed up to the crew of the *Adventure*. At Blackbeard's orders, his crew pulled the ropes tight. Although he couldn't make out the words, Aaron heard shouting back and forth between both ships. The *Queen Anne's Revenge* did not budge, but the distance between the two boats grew less and less with each passing moment, and Aaron and Thomas stood watching, mouths agape, as the *Adventure* also crashed into a sandbar.

Richards immediately ordered the *Revenge* to hang back even farther, and the *Caesar* did the same. The *Queen Anne's Revenge* sent an anchor out in a small boat. They dropped it and the crew tried in vain to pull the ship from the sandbar.

86

Blackbeard himself finally climbed into a smaller boat and visited the captains of the *Caesar* and the *Revenge*. Shortly after, men from these ships commenced launching smaller boats to shuttle the crew off the two stranded vessels and onto the two that remained operable.

Thomas and Aaron immediately hopped into a boat and rowed directly to the *Queen Anne's Revenge*. Thomas scaled up the side as pirates dropped into the boat, and when no more could fit into the small craft, Aaron rowed them back to the *Revenge*.

After depositing the men, Aaron returned quickly to Blackbeard's ship. As he approached it, he looked up and spotted Thomas and Jonathan waving to him. He smiled and waved back as he pulled alongside the *Queen Anne's Revenge* to pick up the next load of men. Stede Bonnet and David Harriot were in the middle of an argument when they dropped the ropes into the boat. Harriot's face was beet red, and a string of curses flowed from his mouth. He waved an arm furiously before descending into the shuttle.

"Don't *tell* me it wasn't on purpose!" the former captain of the *Adventure* yelled.

"Keep your voice down," Bonnet hissed, motioning with his hand.

"Why?" Harriot argued. "I've got nothing left to lose—my ship is ruined and he did it *intentionally*."

Bonnet heavily plopped into a seat at the bow, his eyes never landing on Aaron but instead meeting Harriot's gaze boldly. "You're being ludicrous, Captain," he said, wiping his forehead with a silk handkerchief. "Why would he ruin two ships intentionally?"

"Do you think he doesn't know this area? He's been to Topsail Inlet before. He knew *exactly* where that sandbar was and he headed straight for it!"

"Why?" Bonnet asked again. "Why would he purposefully wreck two ships?"

"To lighten his load, you incompetent imbecile," Harriot growled. "Every ship in the Royal Navy is after us now . . . looking for a French-built four-masted square-rigger with three smaller ships. He's getting rid of his liabilities—and in case you don't understand what that means, that means *us*!"

"Not true!" Bonnet said quietly, but Aaron saw a shadow of doubt flit across his face. "He has always wanted to privateer—he only turned pirate when the war ended and he was left with no other choice." Bonnet tucked the handkerchief away dismissively. "Now that rumors of war are surfacing, he can't wait to get back to serving as a privateer again! He told me so himself before we ever wrecked."

"Are you *insane*?" Harriot asked, his eyes widening. "He's not going to return to being a privateer. He's lying to you!"

Bonnet stuck out his chin. "Preposterous! He's going to Bath to seek amnesty. He's even offered to stay and ready the *Revenge* and keep an eye on things while I go receive my commission to privateer against the Spaniards as well. When I return, I'll do the same for him."

"He's sending you up there first to see if you come back alive," Harriot warned.

They were already approaching the *Revenge*. Bonnet reached up to the rope ladder, grabbed hold of the rungs and looked up lovingly at his ship.

"Nonsense," Bonnet said, sticking one black boot into a rung. "We're going to privateer together. I'm sorry your *Adventure* was lost, but I recommend you join us."

"I believe I'll wait and see if you come back alive," Harriot said hotly, grabbing hold of the ladder behind Bonnet.

Aaron's next load of men was made up of sailors who, like Jonathan and Thomas, had originally been on the *Adventure* when she was captured by Blackbeard.

"I'm telling you, Charles," one of them whispered conspiratorially to another. "This is it . . . *this* is our chance."

"I don't know," the young man Aaron assumed was Charles answered hesitantly.

88

"That's the mainland, *right in there*," another of them said, pointing emphatically to an opening between the two islands that Blackbeard had been headed toward when he wrecked.

"There's not room for all these men on only two ships!" a fourth man agreed. "No one's going to come after us . . . rather I think they'll be happy to see us go."

"I think they're right, Charles," the man sitting closest to Aaron said, nodding.

"Maybe," Charles replied, although he still did not sound convinced.

"I imagine they'll start taking men in to Beaufort before nightfall—we can see what happens," the first sailor offered. "If it looks like there's good opportunity . . ."

Charles nodded, seeming to warm up to the idea a little more. "Perhaps you're right," he admitted. "We'll see how things look when we get to shore."

A familiar feeling of sadness suddenly engulfed Aaron.

"Is it a busy port?" Aaron asked.

The men looked at him with surprise, as if they'd forgotten he was there. "It's not terribly populated," the deckhand sitting to Aaron's right answered. "But there are enough people around that we should be able to slip away, undetected. Do you want to come with us?"

Aaron shook his head.

"Will you cause trouble for us?" another asked, pulling a knife from his scabbard and thrusting it toward Aaron.

"Oh! N-No," Aaron stammered, "not at all."

"Put that away," Charles demanded. "He's just a kid." Charles looked at Aaron. "You're friends with Jonathan and Thomas, aren't you?"

Aaron nodded. Upon learning this, they all seemed to relax.

"He won't cause us any trouble," Charles assured the others as they reached the *Revenge*.

Charles turned to Aaron before he climbed the ladder. "Best of luck to you."

"The same to you," Aaron replied, heading back to the *Queen Anne's Revenge*.

His strokes with the oars were slow now and had lost the rhythmic pattern they'd had during his first few trips. Onlookers might think he was tiring, but he knew it was the result of the turmoil battering his mind.

He sighed as he rowed and replayed the sailors' conversation in his head. Their plan to escape. Could Thomas and Jonathan simply "slip away undetected" and find a new life?

If their chance arises now, he told himself, *I will do everything I can to ensure that Thomas and Jonathan get away safely.* The resolve behind the promise engulfed his mind, his strokes regained their original strength and rhythm, and he smiled to himself.

He was a good friend after all.

He was hoping to pick up Jonathan and Thomas in his next load so that he could share with them what he had learned and help them start making plans, but other men whom he did not know boarded and pushed the boat from the *Queen Anne's Revenge* before he could even look for Jonathan and Thomas.

"Care for a break?" one of the men asked.

"Thank you," Aaron said, turning the oars over to him. He sat down and surveyed the waters around him. Another small boat—not far from them—was also shuttling sailors from the *Queen Anne's Revenge*. Aaron was surprised to see Jonathan on board, waving at him.

Aaron waved back and then spied Thomas, sitting on the other side of Jonathan. He was talking to the oarsman and Aaron looked carefully, squinting until what he thought he saw he was sure of.

The oarsman was Pell.

Were they arguing? Was Pell going to hurt Thomas or Jonathan?

Aaron continued watching.

No. They seemed to be carrying on a normal conversation, just as any two people might do.

Why was Thomas talking to Pell? What could they *possibly* have to say to each other?

And then Aaron saw Pell laugh. And he saw Thomas lean forward, shoulders shaking. When Thomas sat up he brushed his hair from his face, and Aaron saw that he was smiling. Jonathan was laughing too, but he suddenly seemed to remember that Aaron was nearby for he stopped laughing, turned to Aaron again, and lifted his hand in what Aaron took to be an apologetic wave.

But Aaron turned away, numbed by what he had just seen, and when they reached the *Revenge* he scaled up the side quickly ahead of the others and stormed down into the hold. Aaron paced for a few moments, thinking of Thomas and Pell laughing together, and he grew angrier with each step.

Despite this stinging betrayal, Aaron decided—in the end—that he was still going to do what he had originally resolved. He was still going to help Jonathan and Thomas escape.

But I'm glad they're leaving . . . I don't ever want to see them again.

This thought had barely solidified in his mind before Thomas and Jonathan found him in the hold.

"I think most everyone is going to shore soon," Aaron began coldly, trying to concentrate on his plans to help them escape and not his anger. "The town is called Beaufort. It's not a large port, but the *Caesar* and the *Revenge* aren't big enough to hold everybody . . . it's probably as good a chance as you're going to get."

"I know," Thomas nodded. If he noticed the coolness in Aaron's voice, he didn't let on. "I think the sooner the three of us can get there, the better."

Of *course* Thomas already knew. Aaron felt foolish for having allowed himself to believe that Thomas might value any information he provided.

"We've got to let Mary go before we escape," Jonathan said, stooping beside her.

"I'll help you get Mary out," Aaron said, turning away from Thomas, "but I'm not going with you. You two need to go on without me."

Jonathan stood up and looked at Aaron, cocking his head to one side. "What do you mean, you're not going with us? You *have* to go with us."

"No," Aaron said, talking to Jonathan but swinging his gaze back to Thomas. "I don't *have* to go with you." He could hear his voice growing angry. "I don't *have* to do anything. I can do whatever I wish."

"But it's not safe for you to stay," Thomas said, confusion spreading across his face. "Besides, why would you *want* to?"

"Because I need to stay here. Don't pretend as if you suddenly have a great concern for my safety."

"Of course I'm concerned for your safety. You're being ridiculous," Thomas said, reaching for Aaron's arm.

Aaron yanked away from Thomas with such hostility that Jonathan gasped.

"*Don't* lay a hand on me!" Aaron snarled through clenched teeth.

"What's gotten into you?" Thomas asked, slowly lowering his hand to his side.

"What's gotten into *you*?" Aaron yelled back.

"I . . . I don't know what you're talking about," Thomas began, but Jonathan grabbed his arm.

"Pell," Jonathan said quietly, his eyes attempting to communicate the rest. "He saw you talking with Pell."

"So I was talking with Pell," Thomas acknowledged, his brows still drawn together in confusion. "What difference does that make?"

"You weren't just *talking* to him . . . you were *laughing* with him," Aaron growled, rage burning in his veins as he drew his hands into clenched fists. "I *saw* you."

"Keep your voice down," Thomas ordered in a tone that was beginning to match Aaron's. "I was talking with him just as I'd talk with anybody."

"He's not just *anybody*," Aaron said, his voice shaking, his throat tightening. "Somehow I thought you understood that."

Thomas held Aaron's gaze for a moment and then said quietly, "You're supposed to forgive your enemies."

"Forgive your enemies?" Aaron repeated in disbelief. "If you had any idea what he's done to me, you'd *never* say that to me."

"I know what he's done to you—"

"No, you don't," Aaron interrupted, unwelcome tears brimming in his eyes now, the knot in his throat almost blocking his voice.

"Yes, I do," Thomas said gently. "Your scars . . . I know that Pell gave you those scars."

Aaron continued to stare at Thomas and swallowed hard.

"I know about Rosalie, too."

Aaron felt the blood drain from his face.

"And," Thomas continued, his voice growing even softer, "I know why you followed Pell down here that day he came after Jonathan . . . I know what you were protecting him from."

Aaron dropped his eyes to the floor. Thomas did know.

"Aaron," Thomas said, taking a tentative step toward him. "I *hate* what he's done to you. Trying to forgive him is one of the hardest things I've ever had to do . . . don't you know me well enough to realize that?"

Aaron kept his eyes lowered. The tears that had been brimming finally spilled out, and he covered his eyes with his hands. What brief consolation he felt was quickly squelched by the thought of what lay ahead. Saying goodbye to Thomas and Jonathan would have been much easier if he could have stayed angry with them.

"I'm sorry," he finally managed to say, still not looking up at the other boys.

"I'm sorry too," Thomas said, laying his hand back on Aaron's arm. He left it there for a long moment before Jonathan finally spoke.

"Can we please go?"

"I want to make certain Aaron's not angry anymore. Are we settled now?" Thomas asked. Finally looking up at him, Aaron nodded.

Thomas and Jonathan both seemed relieved.

"Let's go," Thomas said, and he and Jonathan turned to leave.

Aaron stood as if rooted, unable to move or speak. This was the moment he had been dreading, the moment when Thomas and Jonathan were going to find out the truth and their friendship would evaporate.

Thomas turned to him. "Are you coming?"

Aaron managed to shake his head.

"I thought things were all right between us now . . . what's the matter?"

"It's not that. I . . . I just can't go with you. I'll help you get Mary overboard though," Aaron added, "but then you need to leave without me."

"What? We aren't going to leave without you! What are you talking about?" Thomas asked, sounding incredulous.

"I have to stay here and wait for Bonnet."

"Why?"

"Bonnet's going to Bath tomorrow to get amnesty and I'm traveling with him."

"No!" Thomas said, stepping closer to Aaron. "You don't need *amnesty* . . . you haven't even done anything wrong. You need to come with us."

"I'm . . . I'm not going with him to get amnesty," Aaron tried to explain.

"Then just come with us," Jonathan said.

"I can't. I have to go with Bonnet."

"Why would you do that? You don't need to go with Bonnet," Thomas insisted. "*You need to come with us.* We've got to get out of here while we still can."

Aaron took a deep breath and closed his eyes. He had promised himself that he would do whatever he could to make sure that they got away safely, and he could tell they weren't going to leave until he told them the truth.

Say it . . . just say it and get it over with.

Aaron looked at Thomas and Jonathan and in a voice barely above a whisper, he managed to say, "He's my father."

When Bonnet came back to Topsail Inlet, he found that Teach and his Gang were gone, and that they had taken all the Money, small Arms and Effects of Value out of the great Ship, and set ashore on a small sandy Island above a League from the Main, seventeen Men . . . where there was neither Bird, Beast, or Herb for their Subsistance, and where they must have perished if Major Bonnet had not two Days after taken them off.
—Daniel Defoe

~ ~ ~

Deciding to Stay

Their bodies had been turned—half facing Aaron, half heading toward the door—waiting for him to follow. But now they faced him fully, watching as he sank to the floor in front of them and hugged his knees.

"You told me that your father was dead . . . ," Thomas said as he and Jonathan sat down opposite Aaron.

The look of shock on their faces would be etched in his mind forever.

"No," Aaron said, sick over it. "I never actually told you that . . . you assumed it and I didn't correct you. I should have told you, but . . ." He dropped his eyes to the floor. "I didn't want you to know."

"Is your mother alive too?" Thomas didn't sound angry or hurt; he just seemed to want to know the truth.

"No," Aaron said. "I lived with her all my life, but when she died, Bonnet bought the *Revenge* and we left Barbados."

"Why?"

"Because . . ." He stopped, sighed, and looked at his friends. "It's a long story."

The pressing need to go suddenly evaporated. This was a tale they needed to make time for.

"Start at the beginning," Thomas suggested, and Aaron nodded, warmed by his friends' willingness to stay for a few more minutes.

"Bonnet fell in love with my mother when they were both young, but his grandmother didn't approve—his parents died when he was little, and she's the one who raised him. She was always in charge, and she's the type of person who's only concerned with how things *appear* to everyone else."

Aaron took a deep breath and glanced at Thomas' and Jonathan's faces. They sat still, waiting patiently for him to unravel his story.

"Anyway, she didn't think that my mother was the 'right sort' for her grandson. My mother came from a very poor family, and Bonnet's grandmother wanted him to marry someone from a family more like his own. When she found out that they were seeing each other, she forbade him to ever see my mother again."

"So they ran away together?" Jonathan guessed.

"I *wish* that's what they'd done," Aaron said, "but Bonnet didn't have the courage to defy his grandmother. He *always* put his grandmother and her wishes first—never my mother's. His grandmother had some kind of hold over him . . . I don't know why, but he always did exactly what she told him to do."

"So if they didn't run away together, then what happened?" Thomas asked.

"Bonnet's grandmother arranged for him to marry a 'proper' girl from a suitable family. They got married, had children . . . he did everything that his grandmother wanted him to do."

Jonathan frowned. "Then how is he your father if he stopped seeing your mother?"

"He *didn't* stop seeing her . . . ever. He went to visit her secretly whenever he could. He gave her money to support her—and me after I came along."

Aaron couldn't imagine what they were thinking. Their faces gave nothing away. He continued.

"I know it probably sounds as if my mother was an awful person, but she wasn't. She really loved him. I don't know *why* she loved him," he said, almost to himself, "but she did. Most women would have wanted more—but it never seemed to bother her that he spent the majority of his time with another family. She always seemed happy with whatever time he could spare for her."

"And were *you* happy?" Thomas wanted to know.

This question surprised Aaron, and he thought for a moment, absently tracing the grain in the deck beneath him.

"I was happy," he finally decided. "I knew that Bonnet was my father, but he was hardly ever there. That was the way I grew up—it was what I always knew."

Whenever Bonnet had come to visit, he almost acted as if he was surprised to see Aaron—as if he had somehow forgotten his existence. But Aaron didn't mind. If Bonnet had quit coming around all together, it wouldn't have bothered Aaron one bit, and Bonnet visited so infrequently that it barely disrupted things at home—at least not for long. Most of the time, Aaron had his mother all to himself, and he had liked that.

"My mother was waiting for him one day," Aaron went on, casting hesitant glances at his friends in another attempt to gauge their reaction. "He was supposed to visit her, but he never showed up. She sent me to try to find out if he was coming, but while I was gone there was a fire and . . ."

Aaron trembled, remembering the searing heat, the hiss and growl of flames that met him when he'd returned. He swallowed and looked up at Jonathan and Thomas, feeling his lip curl up in a sneer.

"Do you know where he was?" Aaron asked, not attempting to hide his anger . . . or disappointment. They shook their heads.

"He was at a party! A *party*! My mother was waiting for him and she *died*, and he was at a party!"

He snorted in disgust and flicked a piece of rat dung off into the darkness. "By the time I got back, someone had pulled her out and she was lying there on the ground . . . screaming for someone to help her, but . . ."

He swallowed hard.

"People held me back; they didn't want me to see her. They took her away and she died the next day. Bonnet was able to see her before she died and he talked with her. She asked him to do something."

"To take care of you?" Thomas guessed, and Aaron nodded.

"That's what he said. He said that he promised her he would. He gave me some money and told me to wait—that he'd be back for me when the time was right. I assumed he was going to tell his family . . . his grandmother and his wife and his children. While I was waiting for him to come back for me, I imagined what it was going to be like to live with them, to have brothers and sisters. I wondered how they were ever going to accept me . . ."

"But that's not what he did?" Thomas ventured.

Aaron stifled a bitter laugh. "No," he said, shaking his head, "that would have been the *right* thing to do . . . the *brave* thing: to finally stand up to his grandmother—to tell her about my mother and to demand that I be a part of his family. But he didn't do that. He bought the *Revenge* and told everyone it was for transporting rum and sugar. He hired a crew and brought me on board, and then one night, we just sailed away. I had no idea we were pirating until the first day I saw the black flag."

"He took you and ran away instead of simply telling his family the truth?" Jonathan asked. "How could he just leave them?"

Aaron shrugged. He had wondered that same thing countless times. "I don't think he ever really loved them, and after my mother died I think he grew to hate them," he said, spelling out his theory. "I think he especially hated his grandmother. He blamed her for my mother's death—he convinced himself that my mother's death was her fault."

"How was it his grandmother's fault?"

"It *wasn't* her fault; it was *his* fault, but he said that if she hadn't made him go to the party that he would have been there when the fire broke out . . . that he could have saved her. He could never admit that it was his fault . . .

that if he had just stood up to her—for *once* in his life—she wouldn't be dead right now."

"Why did he decide to go *pirating*?" Thomas wondered aloud. "If he couldn't face them, why didn't he just run away and start a new life somewhere else?"

"I'm not certain," Aaron said, shaking his head, "but I think he just hates his grandmother so much that he wanted to hurt her as deeply as possible. I think that's why he burned every ship we took that was from Barbados. To someone like her? Someone who thought reputation was everything? She probably couldn't show her face in public once word got back to Bridgetown. Her grandson not only left his family but became a *pirate* too? What better way to disgrace her?

"He thinks he did something brave," Aaron finished. "He acts as if he confronted his grandmother or something, but all he really did was just run away from her like a coward. He didn't tell her about me or my mother— he never stood up to her at all."

Aaron's voice trailed off and he looked at Jonathan and Thomas, still unable to read their faces or determine what they might be thinking. He wanted to tell them he was happy for them that they were finally escaping. He wanted to tell them how much their friendship had meant to him over the past few months. He wanted to tell them that he was going to miss them more than they could know . . .

"I'm sorry I didn't tell you the truth sooner, but . . ." Aaron took a deep breath and stood up, walking over to Mary. He suddenly dreaded his future again; he was going to be as miserable as he'd been before meeting Thomas and Jonathan.

They had made his situation bearable . . .

Maybe he *should* go with them . . . abandon Bonnet and start a new life. He wanted to so badly, but something inside wouldn't let him leave the man he called a father.

"Let's hurry up," he said, glancing back at them. "I think that the sooner you get to shore the better your chances are going to be."

Thomas and Jonathan stood up and joined him next to Mary.

"Are you certain you won't leave with us?" Thomas asked quietly.

"No," Aaron said, shaking his head. "I can't."

"Very well," Thomas said, nodding in resolve. "Then we're going to stay too."

"What do you mean?" Aaron asked, stepping back in shock.

"We don't believe you should be here alone with . . . with . . . well, we just want to stay with you."

"You can't do that," Aaron protested mildly, afraid to allow himself to hope that they actually would.

"We're staying with you," Thomas said firmly, and Jonathan nodded in agreement.

Aaron said nothing, for anything that might come out of his mouth would be woefully inadequate. He felt guilty for not being able to express his gratitude, and also because he knew that Jonathan and Thomas were giving up their best chance for freedom, yet he wanted them with him and he was thankful that they weren't going to leave him alone. Aaron found himself smiling, bolstered by their presence.

Thomas and Jonathan were staying, and no matter what lay ahead, Aaron finally felt as if he would be able to face it.

Aaron and Thomas spent the next few minutes trying to convince Jonathan that because of all the chaos occurring around them, this would still be the perfect opportunity to let Mary go, but in the end he couldn't bring himself to say goodbye to her. Instead, they spent the rest of that day and much of the next helping Bonnet get a small sailboat ready for the trip to Bath.

Aaron, along with several other men, accompanied Bonnet as he went to seek his amnesty. Although Harriot had warned Bonnet that it might be a trap, they found the government's offer to be good, and by the time the group left, Bonnet had been absolved of all prior acts of piracy he'd committed.

The entire trip back to Beaufort, Bonnet talked of going to St. Thomas to receive a commission to privateer against the Spaniards. Aaron felt his old optimism returning: his father was not going to be a pirate any longer, and Thomas and Jonathan would be waiting for him when they got back.

But when they reached the place where they'd left Blackbeard with the two remaining boats full of men, they found that the *Caesar* was gone and the *Revenge* was all but empty. A cursory glance revealed that her cannons had been removed, and they climbed on board to discover that anything of any value had been taken and that the ship was completely deserted.

As the tiny crew sailed the *Revenge* downstream toward Beaufort, Bonnet stormed about, cursing loudly over Blackbeard's betrayal, but Aaron stood quietly on the deck of the ship in absolute disbelief that Thomas and Jonathan were gone. What had happened to them? Had Blackbeard forced them to sail away once again?

He closed his eyes.

Please God . . . please let them be all right. Please let them have escaped . . .

Suddenly Aaron heard shouting and opened his eyes to find the two brothers rushing out from a stand of trees before tearing down the shoreline alongside the ship, waving their arms and frantically yelling.

Oh . . . thank you, God.

And Aaron smiled.

"Where's Blackbeard?" Bonnet demanded gruffly once the boys had been brought on board.

"He's gone," Thomas explained, his chest heaving as he tried to catch his breath. "And he stranded a bunch of men near the inlet."

They sailed past Beaufort, and Thomas pointed them toward a small patch of land that was barely more than a sandbar. There they found 20 men, including Pell, Vander, Richards, Harriot, and Bayley, who were already suffering after two days with no fresh water or nourishment. Barely able to stand, they pleaded for water through swollen, cracked lips and Bonnet ordered a handful aboard at a time. After several trips from the island to the boat, all of the weak, pasty-faced pirates had been delivered onto the *Revenge*.

As Aaron and some of the others tried to keep the men from guzzling water, Bonnet muttered under his breath about the size and sickly condition of his crew. The next day, after fully assessing the situation, Bonnet made a trip into Beaufort to recruit more able-bodied seamen. He came across a few who had once sailed with Blackbeard's fleet and were interested in going with Bonnet to St. Thomas, but most of the old crew had either left with Blackbeard or—as Charles and his friends had discussed—simply disappeared into the little community on the mainland.

Bonnet and his small, refurbished crew spent a few days purchasing provisions in the little town, and when they were finished, Bonnet gathered them together on the deck of the *Revenge* to make an announcement that would make Aaron's heart almost light.

"We're to sail to St. Thomas," Bonnet pronounced proudly, glancing around in a self-assured manner that Aaron hadn't seen for months. "There, we will obtain a commission to become privateers. No longer will we follow this evil course of life that Blackbeard has tried to force upon us."

After this, the Major threw off all Restraint, and tho' he had just before received his Majesty's Mercy, in the Name of Stede Bonnet, he relaps'd in good Earnest into his old Vocation, by the Name of Captain Thomas, and recommenced a down-right Pyrate, by taking a plundering all the vessels he met with.
—Daniel Defoe

~ ~ ~

Beyond Revenge

Although they had been following that "evil course of life" since long before they'd met Blackbeard, it seemed to Aaron that his father was taking his newfound amnesty seriously. In an apparent effort to shed his former reputation, Bonnet renamed his ship the *Royal James*, which sounded much more respectable to Aaron than *Revenge*. As they prepared to sail for St. Thomas for their commission, Bonnet changed his own name as well, deciding that he wanted to be called "Captain Thomas," and—although none of the crew could be bothered with either of the new names—the lightening of Aaron's heart continued.

Even more encouraging was the fact that Pell had not bothered him in months—something that Aaron contributed to the fact that it was now evident to everyone that he was friends with Thomas and Jonathan. Although Aaron had once tried to keep their friendship a secret for fear that Pell would try to destroy it if he knew about it, Aaron now believed this friendship was likely the very reason Pell was leaving him alone: Thomas was nearly as large as Pell and easily as strong as well. Strength in numbers, Aaron suspected, didn't hurt either.

Soon after they had set off for St. Thomas, the *Revenge* (or the *Royal James*, or whatever they were supposed to be calling it) approached a merchant ship, and the men expertly took her over as they'd been doing since their early days at sea. Aaron found himself watching in dismay as Bonnet's newly formed crew gleefully removed provisions from the captured ship and he clutched the rail on the leeward side of the boat, trying to keep his face still as panic and disappointment washed over him.

It was a lie . . . all a lie. His newfound amnesty means nothing to him. He has no intention of receiving a commission to become a privateer. He will never do the right thing . . .

But then—to Aaron's amazement and great, sweeping relief—Bonnet *paid* for the items that had been taken.

Granted the ship had indeed been captured, and granted Aaron was fairly certain that the captain of that ship hadn't actually *intended* to sell provisions . . . but still. At least he did get paid.

"It's not exactly stealing . . ." Jonathan, standing next to Aaron, noted in a small voice that echoed his very thoughts. Aaron gave a small nod in reply.

Within the next few days, Bonnet plundered two more ships, and each time, payment was given in exchange for what was taken. Aaron knew that Bonnet wasn't approaching these trades in the most traditional manner, but neither was he downright pirating anymore either, and Aaron's mood remained hopeful.

As they headed to St. Thomas, still pursuing their commission, Aaron discovered he was actually looking forward to his future. Scrubbing pots in a sunny section of the bow, he admitted that he didn't relish the thought of privateering against the Spaniards. Capturing enemy ships on behalf of your country was certainly dangerous, but at least it would be legal work. His eyes wandered down to Bonnet, standing at the ship's wheel, a striking figure of a man in a burgundy coat and coal-black tricorn cap. He was steering and—at last—commanding his ship again. Aaron felt his chest swell with pride. His father was finally acting as if he had some moral character; this alone would have been enough to make Aaron happy. But there was so much more. Thomas and Jonathan were coming too—and not even against their will. They were free now, and they had decided to spend their freedom with Aaron.

He scrubbed some more. And he smiled.

A few days later, Bonnet's ship, anchored far from the North Carolina coast, barely bobbed and dipped in unusually calm aquamarine waters. This rare stop served to give the men a brief reprieve from the rigors of sailing. As they rested, another ship sailed up beside them and anchored. Aaron watched from the crow's nest as Mullet and a few others quickly rowed over to it. Perhaps they knew the vessel and it was just a friendly call; maybe they were getting some more provisions.

Not terribly concerned, Aaron climbed down so he and Jonathan could head below to retrieve a bag of marbles, as the two intended to take advantage of the peaceful water. Thomas waited above board, however, curious, and the boys had barely begun their game on the galley floor when he barged in. Aaron saw immediately that his friend didn't look happy.

"Blackbeard's on Ocracoke," Thomas announced grimly. The low light in the hold added an ominous edge to his words.

Aaron looked at him, puzzled. *Ocracoke was a long way off . . . how could this possibly affect them?*

"I think we're turning around," Thomas continued, answering Aaron's unspoken question.

A sickening feeling launched through Aaron's stomach as he and Jonathan rose quickly to their feet, marbles rolling crazily away from them.

"Why?" Jonathan asked.

Thomas set his jaw. "Revenge," he said. "The crew wants revenge."

Thomas was right. The crew almost immediately voted to return to North Carolina to find Blackbeard. The marooning was still fresh in their minds and Bonnet's humiliation wasn't forgotten, either. They were all going to make him pay.

But when they arrived at Ocracoke, Blackbeard was gone. They had missed not only him but also their opportunity to get even.

"He can't be far!" Lopez shouted.

"Let's think like Blackbeard," Mullet muttered from beside Aaron. They stood beside each other at the rail, looking out over the flat, featureless sea of marsh and grass. "Where would he have gone next?"

"Why don't we sail north," Vander suggested from behind them. "We'll stop at Norfolk and see what the word is there."

Bonnet, standing farther down the railing, aloof and separated from the men, said nothing. His eyes searched the barren landscape. Aaron looked at him, waiting for him to take charge, to tell them they didn't have time to go chasing after Blackbeard anymore. But moments passed in silence as Bonnet merely clasped his hands behind his back.

Do something. This is ridiculous. We're sailing to St. Thomas. We're going to get a commission . . . do *something.*

But once again, Bonnet let Aaron down.

As the days went by, the crew sank deeper and deeper into the lifestyle they had all grown so accustomed to. Soon there was no payment for items taken from unwary ships that innocently passed by. They stole whatever they could whether they needed it or not, and Bonnet took his shares each time. They captured a schooner off the coast of Virginia, and Bonnet ordered that she be kept as tinder; as the two ships sailed together across the steel blue waters of summer, there was no more talk of going to St. Thomas.

Bonnet had spent months watching Blackbeard manipulate his crews and wield tyrannical power over anyone who crossed his path, and Aaron watched as Bonnet now began experimenting with some of those same techniques himself. The crew, however, did not respond to

Bonnet's efforts with the same respect they'd afforded Blackbeard—instead his barbaric and outrageous behaviors were merely met with sidelong glances and sneers. Much to Aaron's horror, however, Bonnet soon discovered that if he used his cruel tactics on the *victims* of their pillaging, the crew gave him the type of response he had been looking for: cheering and laughing at their captain's merciless brutality.

Soon it became routine for Pell to bring the captain of their latest prize onto the *Revenge*, where Bonnet would scrutinize his prey. Quietly he would admire something about the man, such as his wig, and then violently rip it off, or cast a compliment about his gold ring and then remove it with a knife—finger and all. The more Bonnet was able to harm and humiliate his victims, the better his crew responded to him. Pell and Vander especially seemed to appreciate the new Bonnet, and Bonnet went out of his way to please them.

And one day, he took it too far.

The two pirate ships came across a passenger ship heading out of Boston. Warning shots were fired, a Jolly Roger hoisted, and the pirates began seizing trunks, throwing them carelessly onto the deck of the *Revenge*.

Aaron went below deck. Bonnet usually ordered him there anyway whenever they took a ship, so as soon as he'd realized what was getting ready to occur he had sullenly resigned himself to it and slipped down the hole. But soon he heard crying . . . a woman crying. Almost involuntarily, he followed the heart-wrenching sounds to Bonnet's cabin and peered in, startled to see three passengers: a man, a woman, and a young boy.

The woman—although Pell was holding a knife to her throat and her eyes were red from tears—was beautiful. She had delicate, gentle features awash in golden curls, and she was pleading for the life of her son. The boy was probably eight or nine years old, and Bonnet was grasping the boy by the hair with one hand and holding a knife in the other. The child, as blonde as his mother, looked more confused than actually afraid. Vander held the man, who stared at Bonnet through round eyes brimming over with fear. The man was clearly the father and obviously aware of how much danger they were in. Aaron glanced back at the woman, a desire to help her burning in him like nothing he had ever felt before.

He could tell just what kind of a mother she was, even from this quick glimpse. She would do anything for her son. He meant more to her than anything. She spent all her time doing things for him—sewing his clothes, cooking his meals, tending to his every need. Somehow, Aaron was sure of it.

He imagined her and the boy bent over a book in front of their fireplace, the light dancing in their fair hair, her hand lightly resting on his shoulder. Gentle but firm. She was relentless as she encouraged him in his studies, prepared his favorite foods, and read to him by his bedside every evening.

"Please don't hurt Sam," the father begged, barely an ounce of dignity left in his voice. "We'll give you anything you want—anything!"

Aaron took in what he could about the father too. He was a perfect complement to the woman. Strong and tall, he would be the sort to teach the boy how to hunt, or maybe how to farm. He'd take the boy with him when it was time to help a neighbor in need to show him the importance of serving others. This was a man who would always have the courage to do what was right—a father who would give his life for his son without thinking twice . . . Aaron knew this had to be true.

At that moment, Bonnet noticed a gold cross hanging around the woman's neck and his eyes glittered. "Her necklace!" he demanded. Pell ripped it viciously from her neck and tossed it to his captain.

Bonnet studied it for a long moment, turning it over in his hand and letting the chain wrap around his blade. Aaron felt certain that Bonnet was going to release the boy as he held the cross, but instead he muttered softly, "My grandmother wears one of these," and then plunged the knife into the young boy's throat.

But the noble man makes noble plans, and by noble deeds he stands.
—Isaiah 32:8

~ ~ ~

Samuel and Hannah Smith

Aaron froze in horror. Both parents screamed and wrestled with their captors in vain as Bonnet dropped Sam's body to the floor of his cabin and, sneering, threw the necklace into the large pool of blood forming at his feet. He pulled a handkerchief from his pocket and strode away, wiping the boy's blood from his hands as if removing a spot of grease. He never even glanced at Aaron. Pell and Vander followed Bonnet, releasing the couple and stepping over Sam's body as his parents dove forward and gathered their lifeless son into their arms.

They wept as they cradled his limp body. The woman looked up at Aaron, sea-green eyes begging him to help her. The grief he saw in her soul jarred him so that he could finally move and—grieving for them ... for himself—he stepped forward and knelt down next to the boy's feet.

"I'll help you," he said, trying to keep his broken heart from choking his voice. They looked at him, pain and confusion etched on their faces. "I'll help you take him back to your ship," he explained quietly. For that was the only thing left to do.

The woman nodded through her tears, and Aaron went on deck to find Thomas and Jonathan. His steps felt so heavy; his chest hurt, as if he'd been kicked. But he tried not to feel, just think. He found his friends and briefly explained what he needed them to do. Jonathan didn't move; the color drained from his face and he simply stood frozen to the spot.

"I'll help," Thomas said. "Jonathan should stay here." He turned to his little brother. "Go on," Thomas said quietly. Jonathan managed to nod and back away.

Thomas and Aaron wrapped Sam's body, so small and thin, in a quilt and carried him as gently as they could onto the other ship. The boy looked only as if he was sleeping, and Aaron hoped he was at peace.

Neither he nor Thomas said a word to each other, and the sailors they passed with the sad cargo fell silent, some dropping their gaze. When they had laid Sam on the bed in the captain's cabin, they went back to their ship, and Aaron returned alone to where Sam had died. He stooped down, lifted the bloody cross from the tacky stain on the floor, and wrapped his hand tightly around it, squeezing his eyes shut . . . trying to forget that moment when his own father had ended the boy's life.

Feeling sick, Aaron went above deck. Duty accomplished, the pirates had released the passenger ship and she was sailing slowly away. Aaron watched for a moment and then turned to examine the trunks that had been taken from the ship before Sam was killed. The men had already rifled through them, taking anything of value. Aaron stopped before one when he spotted a small black velvet jacket—just Sam's size. He knelt to examine what was left in the trunk. He found an old Bible, and then he lifted up a dress and held it to his face. Its scent reminded him of something pleasant from his childhood, although he couldn't remember exactly what, and he suddenly missed his mother terribly. He wanted to bury his face in the dress and sob, but not here, not now. Jaws clenched to hold back tears, he headed for the galley.

Later that night, lying in his bed, Aaron examined the cross in the low light of his lantern. Two initials were engraved into the back of it: H.S. He rubbed his thumb repeatedly over the cross, trying to remove all traces of blood.

After a while, Aaron turned his attention to the Bible that, for some reason, he had retrieved from the trunk. He turned to the Ten Commandments and read the passage

112

that he had found so long ago . . . *visiting the iniquity of the fathers upon the children to the third and fourth generation of those who hate me.* If his punishment had been this bad so far, what was going to happen to him now that Bonnet had murdered a child? But that wasn't what was bothering him so. He could take whatever came his way. What he couldn't bear was that look of horror and grief etched so deeply on Sam's parents' faces. This image was seared into his brain. He wanted to make it go away.

He closed the Bible and held it for a moment and then stroked the cover with his hand. It was dull and quite worn, with bits of leather flaking off. The pages were well read, the binding loose and cracked. He turned on his side and laid it down on his bunk. Then he reached for Bonnet's Bible from the shelf above his head and placed it next to Sam's.

Bonnet's Bible was newer—the dark cover gleamed and the pages were crisp and fresh. He looked from one Bible to the other. Finally, he picked up Bonnet's Bible and got to his feet. Gripping the leather cover tightly, Aaron carried it back to the library and slipped it back onto the shelf. When he returned to his quarters, he picked up the worn Bible and leafed through the pages once again, glancing at all the notes written in the margins in such pretty handwriting.

One of the first things he saw inside the Bible was a record of baptism:

S a m u e l S m i t h
§
Baptized: 7/23/1710
Son of Samuel and Hannah Smith
Grace Church, Nassau Island, New York
The Reverend John Poyer.

Suddenly Aaron sat up, banging his head on the low ceiling. But he didn't care about that.
He knew who they were.

He knew their names . . . where they lived.

Aaron's mind raced like a gull on a high wind.

He could find them and return their things to them—the Bible, the cross, whatever might be left in the trunk . . .

He couldn't give them back their son.

But maybe he could do something . . .

Something to help make things right again.

What would ever be enough?

Aaron considered many options and finally decided upon a course of action. By morning he was nothing less than obsessed with the decision he had made, and he shared his newly formed plan with Jonathan and Thomas the next afternoon, whispering quietly to them in the hold.

"You're going to what?" Thomas asked, incredulous.

It was a rhetorical question, but Aaron answered it anyway.

"I'm going to steal everything I can from him," he said, speaking of Bonnet. "Every reale, every doubloon, every jewel . . . whatever I can get my hands on."

Jonathan, squatting down next to Mary, didn't say anything, but Thomas clarified what Aaron had told them moments earlier.

"And you're going to find the parents of that little boy and give it to them?"

"Yes," Aaron nodded. "They'll never want for anything ever again."

"That's not going to bring their son back," Thomas argued, shaking his head.

"I realize that," Aaron said, nodding again. He really did know that, but he had to do something. "I have to do something . . ."

"Bonnet's made a lot of people suffer," Thomas said, "why do you want to help these people so—"

"Their names are Hannah and Samuel Smith," Aaron interrupted.

"Why do you want to help the Smiths so badly?"

"You weren't there," Aaron said. "You didn't see what happened."

114

"Maybe not," Thomas countered, "but I've seen plenty of things that you haven't."

"My *father* did this to them . . ."

"It's not your fault, Aaron."

"I know that. I know it's not my fault."

"Nothing is ever going to make it up to them for what he did."

Aaron knew that too. He knew in his heart that he would never be able to undo what had happened. But it wasn't about erasing what Bonnet had done. And it wasn't about protecting himself from whatever retribution was about to come his way. It was about Hannah and Samuel, and about an overwhelming desire he had to speak with them . . . to know that they didn't hate him . . . to see their faces . . . the need to know that—despite what had happened—somehow they were going to be all right.

He would never be able to explain to Thomas.

"It's just something that I have to do."

"It's wrong to steal—" Thomas began.

"You can't be serious," Aaron interrupted again. "It's not his money to begin with. I'm just giving back to some of the people he stole from . . . there's no way that can be wrong."

"I don't know, Aaron . . . ," Thomas trailed off.

"As a matter of fact," Aaron continued, waving his hand in the air to indicate the other men on board, "*all* of them should contribute. Every one of them is as guilty as Bonnet."

"Now wait a minute—" Thomas began, but Jonathan suddenly looked up from Mary and interjected himself in to the discussion.

"I'll help," he declared, rising to his feet. "I think it's a good idea."

"Absolutely not!" Thomas cried in dismay.

But Jonathan moved closer to Aaron and together they looked at Thomas. He stared back at the two of them for a long moment and finally relented with a heavy sigh.

"I don't like this idea *at all*," Thomas said, his eyes darting back and forth between his brother and his friend. "I think this is a big mistake . . . you both understand that . . . right?"

They nodded, and Aaron almost had to suppress a smile. Although there was nothing happy or funny about this at all, the plan seemed so right to him that he nearly felt like laughing. He was doing something—*finally doing something*—to begin making things right.

"Let's see if we can figure out a way to do this," Thomas said, shaking his head, "without getting all of us killed."

. . . they clapp'd their Hands to their Cutlashes. Then I saw we were taken: And I said, Gentlemen, I hope, as you are Englishmen, *you'll be merciful; for you see we have nothing to defend our selves. They told us they would, if we were civil. So I was ordered on board the Revenge with two other Men.*
—*Captain Peter Manwareing, 1718*

~ ~ ~

Captain Read's Son

Their big plan to not get themselves killed turned out to be simply to steal whatever they could from the pirates and not get caught. This was harder than they had imagined because pirates in general were a distrustful sort who kept their valuables well protected most of the time. Thomas and Jonathan sometimes had success when the men had been drinking more than usual. A pirate, unnoticed by his friends, would pass out below deck, only to awaken some hours later missing some or all of his money.

Aaron had more success stealing from Bonnet. He would loiter outside Bonnet's cabin late at night and listen for the sounds of Bonnet's incredible snores. Then he'd slip a skeleton key into the door lock, tinker with it until it clacked open, pause until he heard another snore, and slowly push open the door.

At first it had been easy to steal from Bonnet because Aaron knew exactly where to look. But as his money disappeared, Bonnet's suspicions drove him to find more inventive places to hide it. Sometimes it would take Aaron 20 or 30 minutes to make the effort worthwhile, stalking quietly through the cabin, trying to think like Bonnet. Occasionally, Aaron would realize that Bonnet's snores had ceased and he would freeze, not daring to move and wondering if Bonnet had awakened . . . or was perhaps dead. But eventually, without fail, Bonnet would rattle in a lungful of air so loudly that Aaron would unfreeze with a jump, then continue with his search.

When hiding his money didn't keep it safe, Bonnet started taking a slave with him in the evenings. Unlike Blackbeard, who had often offered captured slaves the opportunity to become pirates, Bonnet and his crew usually forced them into service. This particular slave, a young black African boy who often relieved Aaron of many of his duties in the galley, was now forced to sleep in front of the door to Bonnet's quarters. To say the least, this was no obstacle for Aaron. The boy would wake up, scoot off to the side, and watch Aaron quietly through the cracked door, sometimes pointing to help him find Bonnet's latest hiding place. After Aaron discovered some coins, he would always whisper "Thank you" to the boy. He was fairly certain that the young slave did not understand one word of English, but the boy always flashed back a shocking white grin that contrasted sharply with his ebony skin.

One night the boy let Aaron into the cabin, but hesitantly. They entered the cabin and Aaron started his search, but the slave tugged on his sleeve.

Aaron cocked his head to one side, trying to figure the cause for the boy's concern. The slave pointed at Bonnet, patted his own chest, and then pointed back to Bonnet. Aaron's shoulders sagged. Bonnet was keeping his coins on his person now. If Aaron wanted to take money from his father, he was going to have to find another way to do it.

By the time the two ships sailed north to Delaware, the boys had collected a fair sum of money, but nowhere near what Aaron had hoped for. Thomas and Jonathan refused to take their shares whenever a ship was plundered, and Aaron argued with them constantly, trying to convince them to take what they could get. It made no sense in Aaron's mind that they would refuse to take their shares yet they didn't have any problem stealing.

"I *do* have a problem stealing," Thomas protested one day when Aaron began pestering him about it again. The boys were whispering behind some whiskey barrels that had been freshly loaded onto the *Revenge* but were still waiting to be moved below.

"Then why are you doing it?" Aaron asked.

Thomas opened his mouth to speak but then shut it again and walked away.

"Why?" Aaron turned to Jonathan. "Why do you do it?"

"We want to help you . . ."

"Well it would *help* me if you two would take your share!"

"No!" Jonathan said.

"Why not?"

"No one knows that we're stealing, but if we took our share . . . well, then everyone would see us doing that."

"*So?*"

"We . . . we don't want them to think that it's right."

Aaron was dumbstruck. He actually took a step back, as if that would provide a clearer view of his friends' reasoning. "Let me make certain that I understand you correctly," he said slowly, rubbing his forehead. "You're trying to . . . to *set a good example*? For *pirates?*"

Jonathan looked at him, brown eyes wide and innocent, and nodded slowly.

Aaron didn't know what to say, so he said nothing. He never again tried to persuade them to take their share, even though their thinking was ludicrous to him. Instead he busied himself daily by imagining the looks on Hannah's and Samuel's faces when he found them and explained why he was there, and he remained grateful that Thomas and Jonathan were at least helping him as much as they were.

In Delaware Bay they captured two ships in three days—the *Fortune*, captained by Thomas Read, and the *Francis*, captained by Peter Manwareing. Bonnet ordered that Read and Manwareing be brought on board, and they were taken to Bonnet's quarters where a guard stood outside to make sure they stayed put. Jonathan immediately fell back into his old role of serving three men in the captain's quarters as he had done when Blackbeard had forced Bonnet and Harriot to sail with him.

"Manwareing's doing all right," he reported to Thomas and Aaron, down the hall from the guard, "but I'm worried about Read. He's scared stiff. I keep telling him he'll be all right, but . . ."

"But what?" Thomas asked.

Jonathan lowered his voice to a whisper. "His son is on board."

Fury ignited Aaron's blood.

Not again. Not *again.*

He didn't wait to hear another word. Blinded by fear and anger, he tore away from his friends and made for the *Fortune*, boarding it with grim determination, and stalked through the ship, searching until he startled a young boy, about six or so, lying on a bunk.

"Hi," Aaron said in a quiet voice. He smiled at the boy as he knelt down next to him.

"Are you Captain Read's son?"

The boy nodded, eyes wide and round like biscuits.

"Is your mother on board?"

The boy shook his head.

"Who's with you?"

The boy pointed to a darkened corner. Aaron turned and saw a woman edging out of the shadows.

"What do you want?" she asked in a trembling voice.

Ignoring the question, Aaron stood up.

"Are there any other children on board?" he asked.

"No," she told him softly.

"Any other women?"

She shook her head.

He returned quickly to the *Revenge* with just as much determination and headed immediately for Bonnet's quarters.

"Come with me," Aaron said as he walked past Thomas and Jonathan. He knew they would. Faithfully and without question, they fell in step behind him.

120

Aaron burst into Bonnet's quarters without knocking. Manwareing and Read looked up, startled, and Bonnet spun around.

"I'm rowing ashore," Aaron said, surprised at how strong his voice sounded.

Bonnet opened his mouth to speak, but Aaron wasn't finished.

"There is a child on that ship and a woman. We're taking them to shore."

As if on cue, Jonathan and Thomas stepped forward on either side of Aaron.

Bonnet's brows rose. With obvious surprise, he regarded them for a long moment before deciding how to answer. Then, the surprise faded to what looked like suspicion. Raising his chin, apparently so he could look down his nose at the boys, he said, "You'll take Pell and Vander with you then."

"That's fine," Aaron replied firmly. Bonnet wasn't going to scare him out of this. Thomas and Jonathan followed him as he marched out the door.

"What's gotten into you?" Thomas asked as they emerged onto the deck.

"I'm not letting it happen again," Aaron said, his voice now quavering. He was walking so fast they could hardly keep up with him.

"I'm not complaining," Thomas said. "I'm just . . . surprised. I've never seen you stand up to him before."

"You haven't seen me do this before either," Aaron said as he walked up to Pell and tapped him on the shoulder.

"Get a boat ready," Aaron told him. "We're rowing ashore and Bonnet wants you and Vander to go with us."

Pell turned slowly toward Aaron, set his jaw, and stared at him for a moment. Aaron wondered if he had pushed his luck too far, but it didn't matter. Pell could have pulled a pistol and stuffed it into Aaron's mouth and it wouldn't have mattered—he wasn't going to watch another boy die.

Pell glared at him for another second and then, with a disdainful smirk, finally turned and set off to find Vander.

"Let's go," Aaron said to the brothers before leading the way to the *Fortune* to retrieve the woman and Read's son.

As they readied the rowboat and their passengers to leave, Bonnet walked to the rail and looked down at Read's son and the woman.

"If anything happens to my men," Bonnet said in that dangerously calm voice Aaron had come to loathe, "anything at all, I shall burn the *Fortune* and kill your Captain Read."

His cold stare turned to a glare and he shifted his gaze from Read's son to the woman. "And then I'll come into town and burn everything there as well. Do I make myself clear?"

Before Thomas pushed the rowboat off, the woman and boy nodded miserably at Bonnet, but Aaron knew that the message hadn't been directed at them. He wanted to glare at Bonnet but held his face like stone. It would do no good to let Bonnet read too much in his son's face.

Partway through the trip the woman clucked her tongue at Jonathan and Aaron.

"Boys your age . . . *pirating*. You should be ashamed of yourselves."

Pell pulled out his pistol and grabbed Read's son by the back of his shirt. He dared the woman with his eyes to continue talking.

"Don't!" Aaron said through clenched teeth, glaring at Pell.

Pell looked back at him and then shrugged, leveling his eyes on the woman. "Seems like someone would be appreciative when their life has just been saved."

She pressed her lips together tightly and didn't speak anymore.

Aaron looked intently at Pell for a moment, watching as he holstered his pistol. Pell adjusted his hat, noticed

Aaron staring at him, and glared back. Aaron turned away and took over rowing for Jonathan.

Jonathan Clark and one John Dalton came in from South Carolina: they went away from the Sloop; and then after some days, Clarke returned again, but it was with Hunger, tho he said then it was not.

—Ignatius Pell, 1718

~ ~ ~

Cape Fear

They deposited the woman and child safely on shore, and when they returned, they discovered that Bonnet had decided to take Manwareing's *Francis* and Read's *Fortune* with him as they headed south again.

Sitting on the counters in the galley, the boys discussed the situation. "He's got himself a little fleet just like Blackbeard did," Jonathan observed thoughtfully.

"Yes," Thomas said, "but Blackbeard's fleet didn't have to be coerced every step of the way."

Indeed, Bonnet would have to shout through his speaking trumpet periodically at one ship or the other, ordering that if they didn't keep up or if they tried to escape, he would sink them.

By the time they reached the coast of North Carolina, the *Revenge* was leaking badly and the three ships headed up the Cape Fear River. When the tide went out and they saw the underside of the ship, it was obvious that it would be a month or more before she would be ready to sail again. Resigned to the fact that they were going to be there for a while, the men set up a camp along the shore.

Aaron didn't like the camp. The growth in the forest was so dense and overgrown that they could barely move outside of the little clearing they had made for themselves. Not to mention, the mosquitoes were big enough to drain the blood from a small dog. He wanted to stay on the *Revenge*, but she tilted so badly with the tides that remaining on her was next to impossible.

"Trouble," Thomas said ominously one afternoon after they had been in camp for only a few days. He'd risen to his feet and was watching a shallop sailing up the river at high tide, right toward their encampment.

Bonnet lost no time running up a black flag and firing at the small ship. She surrendered immediately, and Pell, Mullet, and Timberhead boarded her, quickly returning with new captives.

Several men were dragged into camp and thrown at Bonnet's feet. Sitting on a log, he casually crossed a knee and forced the captives to introduce themselves as if this were a very civil affair.

"Jonathan Clarke."

"John Dalton."

The first two men glanced around furtively while the others stated their names. Jonathan Clarke settled a defiant gaze on Aaron, Thomas, and Jonathan, all seated on the ground to Bonnet's right. Ashamed, Aaron dropped his eyes to the white sand and wished he could bury himself in it.

"One . . . two . . . three . . . four . . ." The stone skipped and skipped. Jonathan pumped his fist in the air. "Four!"

It was the next day and they were standing near the shore, knee-deep in the water with their pants clumsily rolled up.

"I can beat that," Aaron said, grabbing a stone from the bottom. He took careful aim and threw it along the water's surface, where it promptly splashed and sunk. Thomas and Jonathan laughed.

"You need to hold it like this," Thomas said, wrapping his hand around a smooth, flat stone.

"I know how to skip rocks!" Aaron said.

"Are you certain?" Thomas said. "Because so far, all I've seen you do is—"

"Yes, I'm certain," Aaron said, smacking the water hard with a flat palm and soaking Thomas in the face. He reached for another rock, but before he could throw it

Thomas had lunged at him and pushed him under the water.

Aaron came up sputtering and dove toward Thomas. Jonathan, who had sneaked up behind his brother, jumped on his back. Whooping and hollering, he and Aaron tossed Thomas into the water with a mighty splash.

Thomas emerged and wheeled around to face Jonathan, who was laughing and shrieking but clawing at the water in an attempt to get away from him. Thomas latched onto his waist and was just about to snatch him back into the water when Bonnet's voice boomed from the shore.

"Get out!"

Thomas released Jonathan. The laughter died on their lips, and they all three tramped sullenly toward the shore.

"Dalton and Clarke have escaped," Bonnet said. "Start searching."

They spent the afternoon trudging through thick woods, getting cut with briars and caught in vines. It was futile from the beginning—they could barely walk in these woods, much less find someone, even if they had really wanted to. After several hours of searching, it was evident that Dalton and Clarke were not going to be found. Bonnet finally called off the search with a string of epithets aimed at the escapees.

"Where do they think they're going to go around here?" Jonathan wondered quietly, staring into the dark woods.

Thomas shook his head and Aaron shuddered. He wouldn't want to be traipsing about in this desolate forest, fighting for each inch of movement and getting shredded by thorns every step of the way.

There were plenty of slaves to do the necessary work on the *Revenge*, and they used Dalton and Clarke's shallop for parts. Thomas usually kept himself busy working alongside the slaves, even though Bonnet had never ordered him to do so. Jonathan and Aaron stayed in the shade of the camp, slipping occasionally into the river in an effort to cool off. It was boring, to be sure, but neither of them had any desire to hang off the side of the ship with Thomas, working like a slave.

A few days into this repair mission, Jonathan was riffling through the duffle he shared with Thomas when he pulled out a book, laid it aside, and peered back into the bag.

Aaron picked the book up and looked at the title. *The Pleasant Historie of the conquest of the West India, now called new Spayne . . .*

"Why are you reading this?" Aaron asked.

"I'm not. It's Thomas'."

"Why is *he* reading it?"

"I don't think he is really. It was written by our great-grandfather and Thomas just . . . you know, he just has it."

"Your great-grandfather wrote this?" Aaron asked, flipping through it. There were a lot of words. "I'm impressed."

"Well, he didn't actually write it . . . he translated it."

"He translated it?"

"He was fluent in Spanish. It was written in Spanish and he translated it into English. See right here?" Jonathan pointed to the cover. "Translated by T.N. That's him. Thomas Nichols. Thomas was named after him."

"I wish I could speak another language, don't you?"

"O, pero si hablo otra lengua. ¿No sabías eso?"

Aaron's brows shot up to his scalp. "Pardon me?"

Jonathan laughed just as Thomas approached the campsite.

"What's so funny?" his brother asked.

"Aaron no sabía que podemos hablar español," Jonathan answered.

"¿Oh realmente? ¿Puede él hablar español?"

"No."

Aaron, his eyes darting back and forth, listened to the strange words.

"Bueno, podría demostrar ser divertido, no podría?"

"Pienso que sí."

"What are you saying?" Aaron asked. He was quickly beginning to feel left out while his friends chattered like squirrels.

"¿Se lo decimos?"

"Eso no sería tan divertido como dejarlo pensar que estamos hablando de el."

They both laughed.

Aaron wasn't enjoying the joke. "That's enough Spanish . . . start speaking English now!"

"¿Quieres empezar hablar en ingles ahora Jonathan?"

"¡Creo que deberiamos hablar español toda la tarde y volverlo loco!"

"Fine. That's just fine. Go ahead and—"

A loud crashing in the woods stopped Aaron in mid-sentence, and they all turned toward the noise as if they were expecting to see a bear or an elephant. Instead, Jonathan Clarke stumbled out of the woods and collapsed at their feet.

Clarke was filthy and bedraggled. His clothes hung in tatters and he appeared half-starved. Thomas and Aaron dragged him over to a shady spot and Jonathan brought him some water.

". . . got separated from Dalton . . . ," Clarke explained. "Nothing to eat . . . drink . . ."

"Don't try to talk right now," Thomas said. "Just drink this."

He handed a cup of water to Clarke, who took it hastily with trembling hands.

Bonnet strode by, stopped, and assessed the scene, looking down at Clarke with dark, glittering eyes. Aaron couldn't believe that his father was wearing a wig in this heat. He wondered if it was cooking his brains.

Hands clasped behind his back, Bonnets pronounced coolly, "Jonathan Clarke, I believe?"

Clarke managed to nod, fear in his eyes.

"Not the best place to escape to, is it?" Bonnet asked rhetorically, looking toward the vast woods. Clarke didn't respond.

"You'll set an example for my crew." Bonnet swung his eyes back to Clarke. "Tomorrow you'll begin work on the ship with the slaves. If you try to escape again I'll kill you . . . do you understand?"

Clarke swallowed hard and nodded.

"But, if you do well," Bonnet turned to leave and spoke to the man over his shoulder, "maybe when we finally set sail, I won't make you governor of your own island."

Thomas had to help Clarke to the ship the next morning and worked beside him throughout the day. Occasionally, he'd help the man into the shade and get him some water. Befriending the man without drawing too much attention to themselves was a risk, but there was a great payoff. By evening, Thomas was full of information.

"They were headed to Charles-Town," he told Aaron and Jonathan quietly by their own small campfire that night. "Their plan was to make it there and tell the governor where we are. After what Blackbeard did at Charles-Town, Clarke said the governor is determined to put an end to piracy. If Dalton makes it safely back to Charles-Town, someone will be coming after us."

"Do you really think Dalton can make it all the way back to Charles-Town over this land?" Aaron asked.

Thomas chucked a short log onto the fire. "Yes, if he followed the river to the ocean . . ."

"How long do you think it would take him?" Jonathan asked.

"A few weeks maybe," Thomas shrugged, "perhaps a month. Bonnet was right though, this is a horrible place to try to escape."

Aaron watched them, shadows flickering on their faces in the dim firelight. He wondered if Thomas and Jonathan would try to escape if they ever had another chance, or if they would still choose to stay with him. Suddenly his heart ached. He hated to think about them leaving, but they were in such danger, and his mind flashed back to the moment of Sam's death.

What if something liked that happened to either one of them? They had been so good to him . . .

The realization that he was being totally selfish hit him like a hammer blow. If he was a true friend, he would have convinced them to leave long ago—when Bonnet had gone to get his amnesty at Bath.

But he hadn't made them leave . . . he had let them stay with him.

When Bonnet had returned from Bath and talked of becoming a privateer, Aaron had been so hopeful that things were going to turn out all right. But of course they hadn't, and now Thomas and Jonathan were sitting across from him, not knowing when they'd have another chance to leave.

The next time they could escape, they needed to do so. Aaron had to insist upon it. He was going to convince them to take care of themselves, no matter what. He considered bringing it up right then but decided to wait a while. They probably wouldn't have a good opportunity until the ships had set sail again anyway. He could wait until later.

But as the weeks passed by, Aaron never managed to work up the guts to say anything, and by the time they spotted two naval ships approaching from the coast, it was too late.

Dalton had obviously made it back to Charles-Town successfully, and as Clarke had predicted, the governor was going to take care of the pirates once and for all.

. . . they kept a brisk Fire the whole Time they lay thus a-
ground, which was near five Hours . . . and after some Time
capitulating, the Pyrates surrender'd themselves Prisoners. The
Colonel took Possession of the Sloop, and was extreamly pleased to
find that Captain Thomas, *who commanded her, was the individual*
Person of Major Stede Bonnet, *who had done them the Honour*
several Times to visit their own Coast of Carolina. *There were killed*
in this Action, on board the Henry, *ten Men, and fourteen wounded;*
on board the Sea Nymph, *two killed and four wounded. The*
Officers and Sailors in both Sloops behaved themselves with the
greatest Bravery. Of the Pyrates there were seven killed and five
wounded, two of which died soon after of their Wounds.
—*Daniel Defoe*

~ ~ ~

The Battle

Bonnet sent three canoes downstream to investigate. The pirates returned with grave news. Both ships, they reported, were heavily armed, and Bonnet spent the night preparing for battle.

The *Revenge* was seaworthy enough to sail again. The plan was to head downstream first thing in the morning, firing as they went, and sprint for the open sea. All night the pirates worked feverishly, cleaning and loading cannons, preparing pistols and rifles, sharpening swords, and spreading sand across the deck. The sand ensured that the pirates—in their bare feet—would have an advantage over their shoed enemies on a blood-covered deck.

"I'm not helping with any of that," Thomas told Aaron and Jonathan as they reeled in a lugsail. Instead they helped the sail master ready the sails and inspect the riggings.

In the morning the *Revenge* set sail, racing for the open water. She was promptly blocked by the *Henry* and the *Sea Nymph* sailing upstream to stop her.

"Along the shore!" Bonnet ordered from the bridge, trying to avoid becoming trapped between the two ships.

The pirates began firing and were immediately met with a torrent of return fire.

Suddenly, a grinding noise reverberated through the air. Aaron felt the ship slow abruptly, propelling him forward into a stack of rope, then the shipped listed drunkenly to the leeward side.

They had run aground.

The tide was going out, and the *Revenge* tilted to an alarming 15 degrees or so. Their hull rose up toward the naval ships. Aaron hoisted himself to the rail and peeked toward the other ships—they were caught in the receding tide as well. One ship was a ways downstream, out of firing range, and sitting at a definite angle. The other was much closer and had tilted with its deck fully exposed to the *Revenge*. Her cannons pointed straight into the water.

Although the *Revenge* had the advantage because her hull acted as a barrier against the assault, her cannons were just as useless. They pointed nearly straight into the air. Cursing his luck, Bonnet clenched the rail and bellowed at his men to fire with muskets, pistols, Chinese fireworks for all he cared—just fire!

Agitated and sweating, he noticed Aaron and his friends. "Below deck now!" he growled at his son, but he grabbed Thomas by the arm and thrust a musket toward him.

"Fire on them!" he screamed at Thomas. "Now!"

"Go!" Thomas nodded at Aaron, his eyes wide as he took the weapon from Bonnet. "Go, Jonathan! Go with Aaron."

"Come on," Aaron said to Jonathan, grabbing his arm. He knew it was what Thomas wanted him to do—to take Jonathan below deck and keep him safe. They glanced back over their shoulders for one last look; Bonnet had shoved a pistol into Thomas' side and was glaring at the boy.

"What are we going to do?" Jonathan asked when they reached the barracks, panic weaving its way into his voice. "What are we going to do?" His hands covered his eyes and he was shaking his head. Aaron paced back and forth, thinking. The sounds of battle intensified above their heads.

"Stay here!" Aaron said.

"Where are you going?"

"I'm going to talk to Bonnet and try to get him to surrender."

"Do you really think he will?"

"I . . . I don't know, but—"

"Thomas!" Jonathon yelled.

Aaron wheeled around as Thomas entered the room. Jonathan raced to hug him.

"Are you all right?" Thomas looked from Jonathan to Aaron. The boys nodded their answer. "We have to go right now!" Thomas told them firmly.

"I'm . . . I'm going to talk to Bonnet," Aaron said. "I'm going to see if I can convince him to surrender."

"He's not going to surrender!" Thomas said. "There's already talk of surrender and he's forcing everyone to fight—threatening to kill anyone who won't. The only reason he didn't shoot me is because Vander got killed right after you came down here and—"

An explosion rocked the ship, throwing the boys into the hull.

"We need to leave *now*!" Thomas shouted.

"You know I can't," Aaron shouted back. Thomas stared at him for a long moment before finally speaking. "Jonathan and I are *leaving*," Thomas said. "If you decide to stay then you're insane!" He started to stalk off but turned around with one last remark. "You're not the person I thought you were," he said, and Aaron saw angry tears gleaming in his eyes.

"Wait!"

If they had to leave, he could find a way to bear it, but Aaron didn't think he would survive if they were mad at him.

"What?" Thomas said.

"You know he's my father," Aaron began. "I can't leave!"

"Why not?"

"He's the only family I have left . . ."

"So what?"

"That's easy for you to say," Aaron said, waving his hand at Jonathan. "You have a family!"

"You're a coward!" Thomas said. "You're just like Bonnet!"

"*I am not!*" Aaron was incensed his friend would say that. "I would never be like him—you *know* that isn't true!"

"Think about it, Aaron," Thomas said, taking a step toward him. "You're acting just like him! He didn't do what he wanted to do—what he knew was right in his heart—because his grandmother told him not to! He did what she wanted him to do and now he hates her for it—he absolutely *hates* her! And what did it get him? Nothing! He lost the only thing that he loved and now he has nothing but hate! Well now you're doing the same thing! You're doing exactly what he tells you to do even though you know it's not right—just because he's your family! You're going to wind up just like him *if you don't leave now!*"

In an instant Aaron saw that what Thomas was saying was true. For years, he had never understood why Bonnet obeyed every command his grandmother gave him. How often had he wished that Bonnet would have just had the courage to stand up to her and do what he wanted? To do what was right?

He hesitated, unsure of what to say or do. How could he even begin to apologize for putting them in such danger? Why had they tolerated his foolishness for so long?

Thomas seemed to realize what was going through Aaron's mind and his eyes softened. "Do you want to come with us?"

Aaron nodded and Thomas grabbed his arm. "Let's go then!" he said, heading up to the deck. "We need to get to the shore."

But suddenly he stopped.

"Where's Jonathan?" Thomas' voice was strained. Aaron saw panic in his eyes.

Aaron turned around . . . the barracks were empty. *Jonathan was gone.*

"We'll find him," Aaron assured Thomas.

"Let's split up—then we'll meet at the camp!" Thomas shouted. "If you find him, just go! Don't wait for me!"

Aaron started toward the library, but halfway there he stopped. Suddenly he knew exactly where Jonathan was. The ship was rocked by another hit as Aaron clambered past the galley and entered the hold.

He found Jonathan, sobbing and tugging on Mary, trying to lift the giant turtle. Aaron knew it was futile to do anything but help. He slipped over to where she was, grabbed her under her shell, and—fighting against the listing ship and gravity—helped Jonathan lift her out of the hold.

Musket fire and splintering wood rained down on them. Moving Mary quickly and safely was even more difficult because the ship was pitching so, but eventually they heaved Mary overboard. She hit the river with a splash as loud as the muskets and immediately swam toward the sea. Aaron wondered for a moment how she knew which way to go.

"Thank you, Aaron," Jonathan said, wiping his eyes with the backs of his hands.

"Jonathan, we have to go right *now*." Aaron looked into his eyes to make sure he understood. Jonathan nodded. They escaped over the side unseen and swam to shore.

"Thomas is going to meet us over here," Aaron gestured toward the campsite. They hunkered down under cover and waited for a long time, wet and cold, listening miserably to the battle in the distance. After several hours, the cannons stopped and they finally heard the snap of twigs and thrashing of branches as someone walked toward them.

"Thomas!" Jonathan shouted as he and Aaron both stood up from their hiding place.

Instead, Lieutenant Richards tumbled from the bushes.

They gasped at the sight of him. Practically awash in blood, Richards was in rough shape. His right arm hung uselessly at his side and his mangled right foot, missing its boot, could barely support his weight. His eyes focused on Jonathan and Aaron for a moment before he collapsed. They rushed to his side and Aaron shook his shoulders. "Where's Thomas?"

"They got him," Richards managed.

"What do you mean?" The panic Aaron had been suppressing for hours surfaced in his voice.

Richards answered in a raspy voice, "Got Harriot, Bonnet, everyone that ain't dead. The crew surrendered and turned the captain over."

None of that mattered.

"Thomas was captured?" Jonathan cried.

But Richards didn't answer and his body began convulsing. They realized he was bleeding profusely from his mangled leg, and Aaron was overcome with sympathy for the dying man.

Just as suddenly as his convulsions started, they stopped and Richards gasped, searching Aaron's face with unfocused eyes.

"Everything will be all right," Aaron told him, knowing full well that it wouldn't be. He cradled the lieutenant's head and tried to make him comfortable as his body gave one final shudder and then fell eerily still. Gently, Aaron slid his leg out from under Richards' head, lowering it onto the leaves. Carefully, he closed the dead man's glassy, gray eyes.

Jonathan, mouth open in horror, was staring at Richards' body and Aaron thought he could see Jonathan's heart pounding beneath his filthy shirt.

"Come on," he said dully, taking Jonathan's arm. Cautiously they moved toward the water's edge.

Peering through the bushes, they saw, to their dismay, that what Richards had told them was true. Thomas, Bonnet, Harriot, and most of the others had been captured. They watched as the remaining crew members were loaded aboard one of the naval ships. As the boat set off down the river, it struck Aaron that everything they loved was heading for the sea that day.

"Where are they taking him?" Jonathan asked tearfully.

"Probably to Charles-Town to stand trial," Aaron explained. "We'll go too."

They returned to the campsite. Jonathan would have nothing to do with Richards' corpse. Instead, he walked over to his and Thomas' belongings and packed up their few possessions while Aaron searched the body.

Knowing that hard times probably lay ahead, and that they were entirely on their own now, Aaron took whatever he could find. In addition to two pistols and a knife, Aaron found a leather satchel with a substantial amount of gold and silver coins and a piece of paper. He looked briefly at the paper, but it was a jumble of letters and one name that made no sense to him. He stuck it back into the satchel.

Convinced that nothing else could be salvaged, Aaron packed their items into an undamaged canoe from Clarke and Dalton's dismantled shallop and turned to Jonathan.

"Are you ready to go?"

Jonathan nodded but started crying again. Aaron reached out and wrapped an arm around him. "Everything will be all right," he whispered, holding Jonathan tightly.

Aaron hoped Jonathan wouldn't realize that, less than an hour before, he had said those same exact words to Lieutenant Richards.

I hope the great Reward of Seven hundred Pounds offer'd by the Government for taking Bonnet and his Master, will make the People vigilant in apprehending them. I'm sure the Government gave frequent and strict Charges to the Marshal for securing him, and ordering Centinels to be placed early in the Evening; and immediately on his Escape, set up all night, sending Hue and Crys and Expresses by Land and by Water, throughout the whole Province, so that 'tis to be hoped he will be retaken before this Service be over. I am sensible, Bonnet has had some Assistance in making his Escape; and if we can discover the Offenders, we shall not fail to bring them to exemplary Punishment.
—*Richard Allein, 1718*

~ ~ ~

Escape

They paddled down the river to the coast until they came to a bustling fishing village. After several inquiries, they were able to hire a boat to take them to Charles-Town, where they secured a room at a small inn. Aaron quickly obtained as much information as he could from patrons in the tavern below. Details weren't difficult to come by; the capture of the pirates up the Cape Fear River was the talk of the town.

"Thomas and most of the others are being held at the watch-house under tight guard," he told Jonathan in their room.

"Can we see him?"

"We can try."

"What do you mean 'most' of the others?"

"Bonnet, Harriot, and Pell are being held at the provost marshal's house."

"Why?"

"Bonnet has special privileges because he was a major in the army . . . plus there's a lot of sympathy for him here in Charles-Town. A lot of the citizens don't believe that he could have possibly done anything wrong."

Jonathan shook his head, and both boys were quiet for a moment.

"What about Harriot and Pell?" Jonathan finally asked. "Does everyone think they're innocent too?"

"No. They're turning king's evidence."

"What does that mean?"

"It means they've agreed to testify against everyone else in order to not be punished."

"Everyone?"

Aaron didn't answer.

"They wouldn't testify against Thomas, would they?"

Aaron looked at the floor and swallowed.

"Aaron! They can't testify against Thomas . . . he didn't do anything!" Jonathan's voice was rising in panic. "They won't lie, will they? Won't they tell the truth?"

Aaron looked back up to see Jonathan's eyes sparkle with sheer panic. "I don't know what they're going to do," he admitted softly, shaking his head. "I just don't know."

They tried repeatedly to see Thomas but were turned away every time by dismissive guards who had no time for children. As the trial grew nearer, Aaron and Jonathan grew more desperate, and six days before the trial was to begin, Jonathan tried to convince Aaron that they needed to see Bonnet and Harriot.

"I don't want to see them," Aaron argued.

"We have to, Aaron," Jonathan said. "You said yourself that Bonnet has special privileges because he's a major! He might be able to help us—or at least tell us how to get Thomas freed. And I know Harriot will do whatever he can to help us!"

Aaron was at a complete loss as to what else to do, so he finally consented. He had never missed Thomas' advice more, but Jonathan had a point about Bonnet's rank. But for the rank to do any good, Bonnet would actually have to do the right thing.

Two days later they were allowed into the marshal's house. They took chairs on one side of a table, Bonnet and Harriot on the other. The two men were still wearing the clothes they'd been captured in. They were gaunt, dirty, spattered with what looked like dried blood, and they reeked of urine. Harriot's peppered brown hair was tucked behind his ears but not tied. Bonnet's hair was tied back but wild strands escaped. He was a mess and the discomfit with his humbling situation showed in his slightly stooped shoulders. Aaron sat, sullenly glaring at Bonnet, as Jonathan began crying and rambling the moment he and Aaron were seated.

"What can we do? We've got to get Thomas out! He didn't even do anything—you know that. Can't you tell them the truth and make them let him go?" Jonathan looked at Harriot pleadingly.

Harriot opened his mouth to speak, but Bonnet cut him off angrily and jerked his head at Harriot. "He's already given a deposition—he and Pell both!"

Jonathan wiped his nose with the back of his hand. "What do you mean?"

"I mean he and Pell already gave sworn testimony—" Bonnet cut Harriot a sideways glance full of malice "—and he didn't tell the truth then!"

"I did tell the truth!" Harriot argued.

"You did not!" Bonnet turned his gaze back to Jonathan. "He and Pell worked out ahead of time exactly what they'd say that would give them both the best chance for acquittal. I heard them planning what to say—that Pell was on the crew of the *Adventure* when it was taken over— as if he hadn't been pirating with me all along!"

Jonathan looked at Harriot, who dropped his gaze to the floor. "You told them Pell was with us on the *Adventure*?"

"I told them the truth about Thomas!" Harriot said, looking back up.

"You did not!" Bonnet bellowed suddenly, causing Harriot to jerk. "You said that Thomas was sailing with Blackbeard when the *Adventure* was taken over!"

Aaron couldn't believe what he was hearing. Once again, he had foolishly believed that things couldn't get worse. An icy dread ran its cold hands over him, squeezing the hope out of his heart. A web of self-serving lies and deceit had been spun here and Thomas was an innocent victim.

"*Please* tell me you didn't say that!" Jonathan implored Harriot. "Didn't you tell them that Thomas was on the *Adventure* when it was captured? That he was forced to join them?"

"I may have indicated that he had been with Blackbeard all along, but I—"

"Do you want Thomas freed?" Bonnet interrupted Harriot.

Jonathan nodded.

He slid his hand across the table, as if reaching for Jonathan, who, startled by the gesture, leaned back in his chair. "I need money," Bonnet said. "If you can come up with a substantial amount of money I can bribe the guards . . . I can get him out."

"We have money!" Jonathan blurted. "Show him Aaron . . . show him what we have!"

Aaron cringed in disbelief, thankful that Jonathan didn't know of the additional bag he'd taken off Richards' body.

Bonnet looked at Aaron expectantly. Slowly he pulled out the money they had been stealing over the last few months. Aaron glared at Jonathan as Bonnet examined the contents of the bag.

"I'll take care of it," Bonnet finally assured Jonathan, pulling the bag toward him.

"When?" Jonathan wanted to know anxiously.

"Tonight."

Aaron bored holes in Bonnet's face and knew he must feel the glare, but his father wouldn't look at him.

"Why did you do that?" Aaron snarled at Jonathan as they walked across the cobblestone plaza of the prison.

"He's going to help us get Thomas out, that's why!"

"You can't trust him! Haven't you learned anything?"

"What else is there to do?"

"We could have used the money and bribed the guards ourselves—I'm telling you that you *can't trust Bonnet!* He's not going to help anybody but himself!"

"I . . . I didn't think about bribing the guards ourselves," Jonathan said, his voice trembling. "What should we do now? What should we do, Aaron?"

"Come on," Aaron said, leading Jonathan back to the inn. "I have an idea."

"What?" Jonathan asked, trying to keep up as Aaron marched down the street.

They entered their tiny, dim room and Aaron headed toward his bed against the wall. He reached underneath it and grabbed the bag he had taken from Lieutenant Richards.

"Look at this," he said, pulling it out and dropping it on Jonathan's bed.

Jonathan looked in the satchel, his mouth dropping open. It contained at least three times the money they had just given to Bonnet. Jonathan glanced up at Aaron.

"Where did you get all that?"

"Richards."

"What do we do now?"

"If nothing else, Bonnet had a good idea about bribing the guards. We can still try it ourselves."

"But what if Bonnet really *is* going to help Thomas? What if he was telling the truth?"

"He said it would happen tonight. If Thomas hasn't escaped by morning then we'll know Bonnet was lying."

"Do you think we have enough?" Jonathan asked.

"I think we have *more* than enough," Aaron said, taking several Spanish coins out of the bag. "Anyone would help us for this much money."

Aaron slid four doubloons toward Jonathan. "Keep these," he said. "We'll still need money for our room and food."

Jonathan stared at the gold coins and then looked up. Aaron saw hope in his eyes for the first time since Thomas had been captured, and a small spark reignited in him as well.

The next day they waited to hear news of an escape, but as Aaron had expected, none came. Toward evening they went to the watch-house and approached the evening guard.

"We've come to see one of the prisoners," Aaron told the guard.

"No visitors," the guard said. "I am certain you've been told this before."

"Well, can you at least tell us if Thomas Nichols is still being held here?" Jonathan asked.

"Of course he is! Why should he not be?"

"Maybe he's escaped?" asked Jonathan.

The guard laughed and Aaron looked at Jonathan, leaning down and talking quietly.

"I think you should let me handle this."

"But I—"

"Remember what happened before?"

Jonathan dropped his eyes to the ground, nodding. Aaron turned back to the guard.

"No visitors under any circumstances?" Aaron asked, pulling out a doubloon.

The guard's eye gleamed. "Perhaps I can make an exception . . ." he said quickly, taking the coin.

"We don't actually need to see him . . . we want him out."

"I want to see him—" Jonathan began, but Aaron shot him a look that quieted him.

"How much to get him out?" Aaron asked, turning back to the guard.

The guard looked at Aaron with surprise and shook his head slowly.

"He's innocent!" Aaron whispered. "You wouldn't be doing anything wrong except to be helping an innocent man . . . you'd be helping yourself too!"

The guard, an older man with weathered skin and bushy eyebrows, looked uncertain.

He's innocent! Aaron said again. He leveled a pleading gaze at the guard for a moment, looking for any sign of wavering. When he thought he saw it, he pulled out a handful of coins and forced them into the guard's hand. He took out two more fistfuls and held them in front of the guard with cupped hands.

Aaron shook his hands so that the coins jingled. "He doesn't deserve to be in there . . . he did nothing wrong."

The guard opened his mouth and then closed it again, his hand clenched around the coins that Aaron had already given him. He looked down at the coins Aaron was still holding, watching them glisten in the lantern light.

"He's really innocent?" the guard asked, one brow quirking upward.

Aaron and Jonathan both nodded. "He's innocent."

The guard hesitated but finally took the remaining coins from Aaron.

"When?" Aaron asked.

"I won't be able to do it until tomorrow night," the guard said.

"Tomorrow night then," Aaron said. He grabbed Jonathan's arm, wheeled him around, and headed away.

"I thought we were going to see him!" Jonathan said when they were out of earshot.

"You'll be able to see him after that guard gets him out. I just asked him about visitors to see if he would take a

144

bribe—to see if he could be talked into doing something he shouldn't do."

"How do you know we can trust him?"

"I don't *know* that we can trust him," Aaron said, "but I *think* we can. I think he agreed to do it because he believes that Thomas is innocent. Well, that and the fact that we gave him more money than he probably makes in ten years."

"Do you really think he'll help Thomas escape?"

"If he can, Jonathan, I think he will."

The next day they were eating breakfast at a crowded tavern when a group of men and women descended on the table next to them. They were talking excitedly and Aaron couldn't help but overhear.

"I heard they dressed like women to get past the guards!"

"Bribery, I tell you. The guards are corrupt!"

"I'll bet the governor was in on it."

Aaron dropped his knife and stared at Jonathan.

"Excuse me, ma'am," he said, turning to the lady who had just spoken. "Has something happened with the pirates?"

"Oh, yes! Haven't you heard? Major Bonnet and another prisoner escaped in the middle of the night!"

Maybe it was Thomas! Maybe Bonnet had helped Thomas escape after all!

"What man? Who was it? Do you know his name?"

"Oh, what was his name . . ." She turned to the man next to her.

"Harriot."

"Yes! That's it. David Harriot!"

Harriot?

"Anyone else?" Jonathan asked. "Perhaps somebody escaped from the watch-house too?"

"Nooo," she said, shaking her head. "And I don't think others will be escaping anytime soon! The governor's taking a lot of criticism for this and he's going to make

145

certain there are no more escapes. Security will be tighter than ever now . . . and they're offering a reward of *700 pounds* to make people vigilant about apprehending them!"

Aaron turned back to the table and pounded his fist on it. "I told you! I told you! I told you! I *knew* we should never have gone to see them! Giving Bonnet money was a *stupid* thing to do! Now that guard will never be able to get Thomas out!"

Jonathan stared at Aaron for a moment with tears spilling out of his eyes and then, before Aaron could say another word, he raced out the door. Aaron chased after him quickly.

"It's all my fault," Jonathan sobbed when Aaron finally caught up with him at the street corner. "He wouldn't have even been caught if it hadn't been for me going to get Mary. It's all my fault!"

Aaron put an arm around Jonathan's shoulder.

It's *my* fault, he thought, but even though Jonathan was almost hysterical Aaron somehow couldn't manage to say this aloud.

"It's not your fault."

"Yes it is! *Yes it is!*" Jonathan cried. "I made you give Bonnet money . . . now the guard won't be able to help Thomas escape tonight. Thomas is going to be killed and it's all because of me!"

People walking by on the street looked at them curiously. Aaron grasped both of the younger boy's shoulders and shook him.

"Stop it! Stop saying that! It's not your fault, it's . . . it isn't because of you. Now stop. This isn't helping at all."

"Nothing's going to help! It's over! Don't you understand? They're going to execute him. They're going to kill my brother and it's *all my fault!*"

Aaron couldn't stand it any longer. He clapped both hands over his face and cried out in a muffled voice, "It's not your fault, Jonathan! It's my fault! *It's my fault!* How do you not know that?"

Jonathan stopped crying and looked at Aaron.

146

"Your fault? How is that?" Jonathan asked, clearly puzzled. Was it possible that he had never considered for a moment that Thomas was in prison because of Aaron?

"If I'd gone with you when Bonnet was seeking amnesty, none of this would have happened!" Aaron shouted. He could feel hot tears running down his face.

"No . . . ," Jonathan said, confusion still on his face. "You didn't make us stay. We *wanted* to stay with you."

"But he'd be *free* right now if you hadn't stayed."

"No," Jonathan insisted again, shaking his head.

"And what about just before you went to find Mary? What if I hadn't stood there and *argued* with him for five minutes before I finally agreed to go with you?" He covered his face with his hands again. "Don't you see?" Aaron cried. "Don't you see that it's *my* fault?"

The tears wouldn't stop and now it was Jonathan's turn to put an arm around Aaron's shoulder.

"It's not your fault," Jonathan said, over and over, walking him down the street. "It's not. It's not your fault."

Mr. Killing, *did you never hear me say I would leave that*
Course of Life?
—*Thomas Nichols, 1718*

~ ~ ~

King's Evidence

Four days after Bonnet and Harriot escaped, the trial
began. Aaron and Jonathan spent that time trying to
convince each other that Thomas would be freed and that
everything was somehow going to be all right, but in reality,
Aaron felt that things could scarcely get worse.

Why did *Thomas* have to get caught? If it had been one
of them instead—Aaron or Jonathan—Aaron was certain
they would have been set free. They were younger than
Thomas and might have been released simply because of
their age. But in the eyes of the court, Thomas was an
adult, and age was not going to be a factor.

Another reason Aaron thought that either he or
Jonathan would have stood a better chance of acquittal was
that neither of them had committed any violent crimes.
Bonnet and Thomas had always sent Aaron and Jonathan
below deck whenever another ship was being seized.
Thomas, on the other hand, had always been on deck while
they had been hiding safely below. What part had he played
in the crimes?

At the time, neither had dared to ask. Now they were
both afraid to know.

Although the trial began as scheduled on Tuesday,
October 28th, it seemed to take forever for things to get
underway. Judge Nicholas Trott, a huge windbag of a man,
was exceptionally fond of hearing his own voice and
prattled on and on forever.

Each of the men was to be tried on two different
charges—one for the piracy of Manwareing's ship and one
for the piracy of Read's. Piracy was defined. The jury was

called and charged with their duties. It wasn't until the afternoon of the second day that the men were finally brought in and asked how they pled.

Standing in a long line, a chain snaking through the manacles at their hands, each of the men pled not guilty. Peering over the handrail, Aaron and Jonathan strained to see Thomas. He didn't look their way . . . didn't acknowledge that they were even in the courtroom, though they sat in the front pew, just behind the prisoners. The men filed out again, chains on their hands and feet clanging loudly, and the trial was recessed for the day.

After two long days and no progress, Jonathan and Aaron were each a bundle of nerves by the time the clerk was ordered to send Robert Tucker, Edward Robinson, Neal Paterson, William Scot, and Job Bayley to the bar. A long course of rhetoric and formality started up again, and Aaron feared they would end up sitting through another full day with no progress, but finally Judge Trott announced that the witnesses would be called.

The first to be sworn in was Ignatius Pell.

"Do you know the prisoners at the bar?"

"I know them all very well," Pell said contritely, his fingers laced together at his waist.

"Please give the Court an account of what vessels were taken after you came from North Carolina."

"I shall begin before that time," Pell said, and he proceeded to recount their travels from the time the *Adventure* had been captured until Blackbeard had left them while Bonnet had gone to get his pardon.

"Were all these men sent aboard of Major Bonnet immediately, or no?" Judge Trott asked.

"No, Sir," Pell said. "They were put ashore upon an island."

"How came they on board the *Revenge*?"

"The boat was sent to fetch them aboard."

Bayley spoke up. "Bonnet came with the boat and told us, as we were on a maroon island, that he was going to St. Thomas to get a commission from the Emperor to go against the Spaniards—a privateering—and we might go with him, or continue there. So we ... having nothing left ... was willing to go with him."

Judge Trott turned to Pell.

"You say all were on shore, and all might have gone up into the country. Pray, what constraints were any of you under?"

"None."

Thomas could have left ... *should* have left. Aaron pushed down the sickening knot in his stomach as Pell continued.

"When we left Beaufort Inlet, it was with a design to go to St. Thomas's for the Emperor's Commission to go against the Spaniards. But the first vessel we saw we gave chase to and came up with her."

"What did you take out of that vessel?"

"We took some provisions out of her. After we had discharged her, we saw another, which we chased and took."

"Were all these men aboard and in arms at the same time?"

"Yes, sir," Pell replied. "All was in arms."

He went on, testifying that all five men at the bar were armed and always ready for a fight as they plundered vessel after vessel, each man taking a share of the goods.

Trott asked if all five men had gone onto Manwareing's sloop and if they all had been armed.

"I cannot say that they were all on board, but they all had their arms ready."

"Did they all appear forward and active? Did none of them show themselves dissatisfied or unwilling to act at that time?"

"No, I don't know but one was as forward and as willing to act as the other. All of them had their arms ready."

Then Trott asked Pell about the next ship they had taken. Pell described how they had taken Read's son and the woman to shore and about the goods taken from Manwareing's sloop.

"Was not there more goods taken out of Manwareing's sloop? What became of them? Did you not share them?" Trott asked.

"Yes, we shared a little before we went to Cape Fear."

"Did all the prisoners at the bar receive their shares?"

"Yes, Sir. I know nothing to the contrary."

"They did not refuse their shares? None of them? Did they?"

And Pell answered no.

The prisoners were offered the opportunity to ask Pell questions, but none of them did. Then Captain Read was called to testify and was sworn in.

"Captain Read, please to look upon the prisoners at the bar if you know them?"

"I know them all very well," Read answered.

Read, questioned by Trott, told a similar version of the events from the time he was taken prisoner until they had sailed up the Cape Fear River.

"You look upon all those men as belonging to Major Bonnet, and they were all active in the taking of Manwareing?"

"I did not see but one acted as the other did," Read replied.

"You did not look upon them to be prisoners, like you and your men?"

"No, sir."

"Do you know anything of their sharing? Did they all take their shares?"

"I know nothing of that, for we were all in the round house and were not admitted among them at that time."

"Did you see them have their shares—each of them?"

"I will not say I saw them have every man his particular share, but they were all together when they did share."

The prisoners were offered the opportunity to ask Read questions, but as with Pell, none did.

Captain Manwareing was next on the stand. He gave a brief testimony of how his ship had been captured by the pirates.

"How did they behave themselves with respect to yourself afterwards?"

"They were very civil to me, *very* civil, but were very brisk and merry and had all things plentiful and were a-making punch and drinking."

His testimony also ended with none of the prisoners choosing to ask him any questions.

James Killing, Manwareing's mate, was the last witness. After he was sworn in, he testified that he also knew each of the five men seated at the bar quite well and his testimony echoed that of Manwareing's and Read's.

Then Trott gave each prisoner a chance to defend himself, asking why they had continued to sail with Bonnet after Blackbeard had left. It was one excuse after another. They claimed they were forced into piracy or that Bonnet had told them they were going to St. Thomas to privateer against the Spaniards or that they were in a strange land with no provisions and had to go with him to survive. They told the judge that it had been against their inclinations to share in the goods off the pirated ships.

When they were through, the long-winded Judge Trott recapitulated the evidence against each man and finally sent the jury to deliberate.

"They plead indeed, that they were forced and constrained to go, but give no proof of it; and therefore what constraint any of them appears to be under, I shall leave to your considerations. Though I think the evidence is very plain and clear, yet I shall not pretend to direct your judgments. I shall only remark to you what the wise man saith, that *'he that justifieth the wicked, as well as he that condemneth the just, even both are an abomination to the Lord'.*"

Two hours later, the jury returned with their verdict.

"Robert Tucker, hold up thy hand."

Shaking, Tucker looped a strand of hair behind his ear and raised his hand.

152

"How say you?" the clerk asked the jury. "Is he guilty of the piracy whereon he stands indicted, or not guilty?"

"Guilty," the foreman's firm voice echoed through the chamber.

And so it went for each of the five men at the bar. They were required to raise their hand and listen as the foreman announced the verdicts.

Edward Robinson?

"Guilty."

Neal Patterson?

"Guilty."

William Scott?

"Guilty."

"Job Bayley, hold up thy hand."

Job Bayley held up his hand—one of the very hands that had packed Aaron's wounds so long ago.

"How say you? Is he guilty of the piracy whereon he stands indicted, or not guilty?"

"Guilty," came the reply from the foreman, and then the clerk ordered the marshal to look after his prisoners.

The court then sent eight more men to the bar, and testimony continued all afternoon. By the time each man had been found guilty, it was dark and the court adjourned until the following morning.

"They found them all guilty, Aaron," Jonathan said quietly as they lay in bed that night. "Every single one of them was found guilty."

"They *were* guilty."

"I know."

Silence.

"Aaron, what do you think is going to happen to Thomas?"

"I think they're going to find him not guilty."

"Really? Do you really think that Aaron?"

153

No.

"Of course I do."

"Good night, Aaron."

"Good night."

Friday morning they gathered in the courtroom again.

"Set William Eddy, Alexander Annand, George Ross, Thomas Nichols, John Ridge, Matthew King, Daniel Perry, and Henry Virgin to the bar."

The crowds attending the trials had grown every day, and on this morning, Aaron and Jonathan had been forced to sit several rows back. They strained their necks and sat up straighter, trying to catch a glimpse of Thomas. He walked to his seat and watched as the jury was called to their place. Again, he didn't look for Aaron or Jonathan in the crowd as the long indictment against them was read. It was as if he was avoiding them—going out of his way not to make eye contact.

"Why won't he look at us?" Jonathan whispered. "Doesn't he know we're here?"

Aaron, equally puzzled, shook his head back at Jonathan and whispered, "I don't know."

The clerk called the first witness.

"Call Ignatius Pell, the boatswain."

After Pell appeared and was sworn, Hepworth addressed him.

"Do you know the prisoners at the bar?"

"I know them all very well."

"Please give to the court an account what vessels were taken after you came from North Carolina."

And Pell began, for the third time, describing their activities after Bonnet had returned from Bath.

Aaron and Jonathan sank down into their seats as Pell told of the ships they had plundered and the goods they had shared.

"Did all the prisoners at the bar receive their shares?"

Pell hesitated a moment before answering.

154

"No, sir."

Aaron's breath caught in his throat in disbelief.

"Which prisoners did not receive their share?"

"Thomas Nichols."

Jonathan clutched at Aaron's arm.

"Did he refuse to receive his share?"

"Yes, sir. After he came to sea he was very much discontented, but he said Major Bonnet had forced him to go. However, he would not join with the rest of the men and always separated himself from them."

Aaron and Jonathan sat up straight with excitement.

Then Captain Read testified about Thomas too.

"He behaved different from the rest . . . he did not join with them."

By the time Manwareing testified about Thomas, Jonathan and Aaron were both on the edge of their seats.

"When he was aboard my sloop, he said he did hope it would be over with him in a little time," Manwareing said, "for he hoped to get clear of them. He looked very melancholy and never did join with the rest when they were carousing or drinking.

"When Major Bonnet sent for him, he refused to go and said he would die before he would fight."

The clerk asked the prisoners if any of them wanted to ask questions of the witnesses.

Only Thomas did.

"Mr. Killing," Thomas said, "did you never hear me say I would leave that course of life?"

Aaron glanced at Jonathan, who was sitting perfectly still, tears streaming down his face.

"Did you hear him say so?" Judge Trott asked.

"When he came aboard," Killing said, "he told me he would give the whole world if he had it to be free from them. When he was on board and Major Bonnet sent for him, he refused to go on board the *Revenge* 'til he sent to fetch him by force. And he told me he would not fight if he did lose his life for it."

Now Aaron could feel tears running down his own face.

"He was not with them when they shared," Killing continued. "He told them he hoped he would not be long with them and he never was at their cabals, as the rest were."

"He seems to be under constraint indeed," Judge Trott said, "and therefore must be taken into consideration."

Then Trott recapitulated the evidence against each man. Addressing the jury, he detailed the crimes each man was accused of. His tone changed when he spoke of Thomas.

"But for Nichols, I think it's plain that he was under constraint and force, for Pell himself declares that he would have nothing to do with their shares and he did hope that he should be not long with them. Captain Manwareing and Mr. Killing, his mate, all confirm the same. And when he was sent for to come on board Bonnet, to go out to fight Colonel Rhett, he refused to go. And when he was forced to go on board, he said he would die before he would fight, and accordingly, went in the hole and did not fight Colonel Rhett.

"So that by the whole course of the evidence, I think it is very clear that he was under constraint and fear. As to the rest, I think the proof is full against them, but I shall leave them to your consideration.

"You know that the innocent must not be condemned, so the guilty ought not to be acquitted. Remember you have the lives of these persons in your hands, and I pray God direct you to give a true verdict."

And for the first time during the entire trial, Thomas looked at Jonathan and Aaron and gave them the slightest of nods and the briefest of smiles.

Everything was all right.

156

But I shall not pretend to give you any particular Directions as to the Nature of Repentance: I consider that I speak to a Person whose Offences have proceeded not so much from his not knowing, *as his* slighting *and* neglecting *his* Duty.
—Judge Trott, 1918

~ ~ ~

Bruised Reeds

The jury soon returned their verdict, finding all of the men at the bar guilty except for Thomas. Jonathan fully expected him to be released immediately, but Thomas was led away with the rest of the men and Aaron practically had to hold Jonathan back.

"It's all right," Aaron assured him. "He was found innocent of the charges involving Manwareing's ship, but he still has to stand trial for Read's ship."

"We took Read's son to shore—surely he wouldn't say anything to hurt Thomas."

It wasn't over yet, but for the first time since Thomas had been captured, Aaron felt a hope that wasn't haunted by gloom.

That afternoon they sat through the trial of the remaining men who were charged with pirating Manwareing's ship. Most were found guilty, although a few other men were also acquitted on all charges, as Thomas had been. The following day was Saturday and finally, groups of men were called to the bar to stand trial on charges of taking Read's ship, the *Fortune*. Each man in the first group was found guilty. The afternoon's session tried a group that included Thomas; Aaron and Jonathan were once again on the edge of their seats.

The testimony echoed that of the earlier charge. Thomas had refused his shares, had refused to fight, was threatened by Bonnet but had said he would rather die before he would fight.

Each man in the group except for Thomas was found guilty, and Aaron and Jonathan could barely contain their excitement, but when court was adjourned until the following Monday, Thomas was led away with the rest of the men again.

"Where's he going? Why aren't they letting him go?" Jonathan asked.

"I don't . . . I don't know," Aaron admitted.

He approached an officer of the court.

"Excuse me, sir? Why aren't they setting Thomas Nichols free? He was found innocent on both indictments."

"He can expect release when the entire trial comes to an end."

"Oh," Aaron said. "Thank you."

He turned to Jonathan.

"How much longer is the trial going to last?" Jonathan asked.

"It won't be too much longer," Aaron assured him, but he secretly wondered. The trial had been going on for four days so far. It had seemed like four months.

They returned on Monday for the first of two more days of testimony, and sentencing finally took place on Wednesday.

A proclamation for silence was made while Judge Trott pronounced a sentence of death upon the prisoners. Aaron scanned the room full of men straining to hear the announcement. No one moved, no one breathed.

"You, the prisoners at the Bar," Trott began, "Robert Tucker, Edward Robinson, Neal Patterson, William Scot, Job Bayley, John-William Smith, Thomas Carman, John Thomas, William Morrison, William Livers alias Evis, Jonathan Booth, William Hewet, John Levit, William Eddy alias Neddy, Alexander Annand, George Ross, George Dunkin, John Dutch, Matthew King, Daniel Perry, Henry

Virgin, James Robbins, James Mullet alias Millet, Thomas Price, John Lopez, Zachariah Long, James Wilson, John Brierly, and Robert Boyd, stand here convicted of Piracy.

"You have been indicted but for two acts of piracy; but you know upon the trials it was fully proved against most of you, that you piratically took thirteen vessels since you joined Major Bonnet, and sailed from Topsail-Inlet in North Carolina.

"So that many of you might have been convicted on eleven more indictments of piracy.

"Besides, several of you were proved to be pirates before that time, as belonging to Thatch's crew; and so were guilty of several piracies committed while you belonged to him.

"You cannot but acknowledge that you have all of you had a fair and indifferent trial."

Aaron sighed. *Was Thomas ever going to be released?*

"As to the crime that you are convicted of, which is piracy, the evil and wickedness of it is evident to the reason of all men: So that it needs no words to aggravate the same; and which is so destructive to all trade and commerce between nation and nation, that pirates are called enemies to mankind, with whom no faith nor oath ought to be kept; and they are termed in our law brutes and beasts of prey.

"As most of you have been Mariners by Profession . . ."

Jonathan tugged on Aaron's sleeve. "How much longer?"

Aaron shook his head; he didn't know, but one thing this trial had taught him was that Trott was more verbose than he imagined any human could be.

" . . . so I cannot but wonder, that being so often at sea, you should not consider the great power of God in creating the same, and His providence in preserving those that pass upon it; and consequently, that such thoughts should not cause in you a dread of His power, and a love of His goodness."

Now he was preaching.

Trott was going on and on, talking of murderers and how they were going to burn in the eternal lakes of fire and brimstone. Aaron looked at the condemned men, searching their eyes, wondering what was going through their minds. They barely moved, and most of them looked down at the ground. The rest stared into space, but Aaron could see some of them swallow every so often, as if they were holding back tears.

Aaron pulled his thoughts back to what Trott was saying . . .

He was telling them to make their peace with God.

"And I wish that what I now say to you, in this your deplorable conditions, may make you all sensible of the greatness of your offenses, that so you may become truly penitent; which if you are, you may get hope for mercy from God. For though your sins be as scarlet, even dyed in blood, yet He can make them white as snow. Therefore if you will now turn unto God by a true and unfeigned repentance, He will not refuse you nor reject you, even now in your great distress."

What was he saying? That these men . . . after everything that they had done . . .

" . . . consider how He invites all them that labor and are heavy laden with their sins to come unto Him, and He will give them rest. He will not break the bruised reed, nor quench the smoking flax. The apostle tells us, that Christ Jesus came into the world to save sinners. And He himself assures us, that He came to seek and to save that which was lost and hath promised, that he that cometh unto Him, He will in no wise cast out. So that if now you will sincerely turn to him, though late, even at the eleventh hour, He will receive you."

He was. Judge Trott was absolutely telling these men that they could turn now to God and ask forgiveness, and suddenly it would be as if they had never sinned.

"Doubt not therefore, but that if you will now sincerely turn to God, He will accept you, and pardon and forgive you your Sins."

160

Aaron glanced at Jonathan. He seemed to be listening intently to Judge Trott.

"Jonathan . . . ," Aaron whispered, nudging him.

"What?"

He hesitated for a moment and then shook his head. "Never mind."

"Thus," Judge Trott said, "having discharged my duty to you as a Christian, by exhorting you to an unfeigned repentance for your crimes, and faith in Christ; by whose merits alone you must hope for pardon and salvation; I must now do my Office as a Judge."

One by one he named the condemned men and ordered that each was to be hanged by the neck until they were dead.

"And the God of infinite mercy be merciful to every one of your souls," Trott said. He then declared Thomas and a few other men innocent of piracy, announcing, "You are hereby discharged."

People drained from the courtroom like fast-moving streams after a summer shower, and Jonathan skirted and darted through men like a mouse as he made for his brother. While Jonathan ran toward Thomas and embraced him, Aaron saw Pell leaving the courtroom. Aaron started toward him, feeling the need to thank him for his testimony . . . his testimony that had saved Thomas. But as he neared, Pell's eyes narrowed as if he dared Aaron to approach. Aaron stood motionless, staring, and realized that some wounds never heal.

And suddenly, the need to thank him was gone.

The next day, the boys were tentatively celebrating Thomas' freedom with a good, hot meal, when word came to Charles-Town that there would soon be another trial.

The two escaped prisoners had been found on nearby Sullivan's Island.

Bonnet had been captured . . . Harriot had been killed.

I once more beg for the Lord's Sake, dear Sir, that as you are a Christian, you will be so charitable to have Mercy and Compassion on my miserable Soul.
—*Major Stede Bonnet, 1718*

~ ~ ~

The Letter

Two days after Bonnet was brought back to Charles-Town, the 29 pirates found guilty of piracy were hanged at the water's edge on White Point. The boys didn't attend the hanging and avoided White Point. The bodies were still hanging there when, two days later, Bonnet's trial began.

Bonnet—washed, shaven, and wearing an ill-fitting but clean tunic and brown leggings—pled innocent and denied everything. His voice, thin but resolute, came from a haggard-looking man. Bonnet was bent, gaunt, but not yet defeated. He sounded very much as if he believed everything he reported. He had been asleep during one of the attacks. He had never ordered that any ship be taken. He had never forced anyone to act against their will. He had not wanted to return to a life of piracy, but his crew had insisted upon it.

There was much truth in the things he said, and for a moment, Aaron found himself questioning Bonnet's guilt. Bonnet *had* said that they were going to go privateering. It was the crew, not *him*, who had decided to begin taking ships again. He had said, repeatedly, that he no longer wanted to act as a pirate.

But in a flash, Samuel's crumpled body flashed through Aaron's mind. Aaron shook it out of his head and listened as the testimony against Bonnet continued. He had been in command of the ship. He had ordered that goods be removed from the ships that they'd taken. He had taken his share of the prizes. He had victimized. Tortured. Murdered.

On the first of the two indictments the jury returned their verdict.

162

"Major Stede Bonnet, hold up thy hand."

Bonnet raised his hand. It was visibly trembling.

"How say you?" the clerk asked the jury. "Is he guilty of the piracy whereon he stands indicted, or not guilty?"

"Guilty," the foreman said. Bonnet dropped his hand to his side, his brow clenched with fear, his face showing nothing but dismay.

Court was adjourned. Bonnet would be tried on the second indictment the following day.

That evening the boys ate in near silence, and darkness was not far off by the time they left the tavern. Jonathan and Thomas turned toward the inn, but Aaron didn't follow.

"I want to go to White Point," he said.

Jonathan looked as though he had been stricken. "I'm not going!"

"Oh," Aaron said. "That's fine . . . I didn't mean you two had to go . . . I just . . ."

"I'll go with you," Thomas said.

"You don't have to."

"I know."

"I'm going back to the room," Jonathan said. He looked as if he might be sick.

"We'll be along," Thomas told his brother, and he went with Aaron. They'd not gone far when he explained to Aaron, "He doesn't like to see people after they've died. He was with our father when he died. Ever since then . . . he just can't stand anything to do with death."

"I don't like death either," Aaron said, shuffling along with his head down and his hands shoved into his pockets. "I just feel like I need to go there . . . I need to see them . . ."

"I understand," Thomas said, and Aaron was glad that one of them did.

It was a good thing Jonathan hadn't come, for it was not a pretty sight. Aaron paced along the line of bodies, staring up into their faces, now hideously purple and swollen, trying to remember each one when it had once flickered with life.

He stopped for an extra-long time and stared up at Dutch, Mullet, and Lopez and then again when he reached Bayley. He didn't know why he'd come . . . what he was looking for . . . what he was hoping for. Grotesque, horrible expressions were frozen on their nearly unrecognizable faces. He couldn't find answers here.

"Are you ready?" Thomas finally asked him.

Aaron nodded. It was almost dark. They headed toward their room in silence, heads bent against a cold wind. When they arrived they found Jonathan in bed. He'd left a lantern on for them, but he was already sound asleep.

"I'm tired too," Thomas said. Aaron nodded. In fact, he was suddenly exhausted. Thomas blew out the lantern and they flopped into bed immediately, but despite his fatigue Aaron found himself staring up at the dark ceiling. He finally rolled over and propped himself up on one elbow.

"Thomas?" he whispered.

"What?"

"Are you awake?"

"No . . . I'm sound asleep."

"I don't believe what Judge Trott said, do you?"

"Judge Trott said a *lot* of things. You're going to have to be more specific."

"About asking for forgiveness at the last moment." Aaron tried to remember his exact words. "That if you ask for forgiveness and you really mean it that you'll be forgiven by God, even if it's right before you die. I don't believe that."

"Why not?"

"I think you have to live a good life . . . do good things all your life. You can't just do whatever you want and then

164

ask for forgiveness at the last minute and expect everything will be all right."

"The thief on the cross next to Jesus did it . . ."

Aaron hadn't thought about that, but still . . .

"So what's the point of doing good if you don't have to?"

Thomas shifted his weight in the dark and Aaron could tell he was propped up on his elbow too, talking softly over Jonathan, who was gently snoring.

"Why were you trying to help the Smiths? So you'd go to heaven?"

"Nooo . . ."

"Well, why were you doing it?"

Aaron didn't answer.

"Besides," Thomas continued. "Do you know when you're going to die?"

"No."

"Well then," Thomas said, "unless you know when you're going to die you can't exactly count on asking for forgiveness at the very last minute, can you?"

Aaron shook his head, but of course Thomas couldn't see him in the darkness.

"You have to ask for forgiveness *now*. You have to be certain that you're ready."

Suddenly Aaron had the feeling Thomas wasn't just answering his questions anymore.

"I believe in God," Aaron said defensively. He heard Thomas flop back down onto the bed.

"That's not good enough."

"What?"

"That's not what I was saying—it's not enough just to believe in God."

"What do you mean?"

"Even the devil believes in God," Thomas answered, and he rolled over and left Aaron in silence to put his mind in order.

Tuesday morning the trial resumed. Aaron expected another long day of testimony, but to everyone's surprise, Bonnet changed his plea on the second indictment to "Guilty," and court was adjourned until the following day.

The boys ate lunch quietly, unsure what to say. Finally Aaron spoke.

"I suppose they'll hang him." It was more of a statement than a question.

Jonathan and Thomas didn't answer.

"It's not as if he doesn't deserve it," Aaron said, thinking about Sam. "It's just that . . ."

"He's your father," Thomas finished for him.

Aaron nodded reluctantly.

"It might be different for Bonnet," Jonathan said. "You've heard all the people in town protesting his trial."

"That's true," Thomas agreed. "The public is very divided about what should happen to him . . . maybe he won't get the death sentence."

"It doesn't matter," Aaron said. "I don't care what happens to him."

But all three of them knew that was a lie.

Despite all the public protest, on Wednesday, Bonnet was sentenced to be hanged, and the execution date was scheduled for four weeks from that day. Aaron found himself wishing it would happen sooner, just so it would be over with. He wanted to forget Bonnet and put him out of his mind. He suspected that Thomas and Jonathan wished it was over as well and knew that the only reason they were making no mention of leaving Charles-Town was because they intended to stay with him as he waited for closure. He didn't say anything about this but was silently grateful.

"I don't want to talk about him," Aaron told Thomas and Jonathan as they moseyed down the crowded street, hands in their pockets. "I don't even want to think about him."

Thomas and Jonathan obliged and kept Aaron distracted; they talked of everything but Bonnet and pirates and hangings. It seemed that it was working; as December 10th drew closer, Aaron had managed to almost forget that his father was about to be executed.

But when a soldier showed up at the tavern asking after Aaron, ignoring Bonnet any longer wasn't an option. His father was requesting to see him.

"I'm not going," he told Thomas and Jonathan.

"You have to go see him," Thomas said. "You'll always regret it if you don't."

"I hate him."

"No you don't," Thomas said. "It just seems easier if you tell yourself that."

"I do hate him! Don't tell me that I don't hate him! I know how I feel!"

Actually he had no idea how he felt; he had never been more confused.

"One last time, Aaron," Thomas said. "Go and see him one last time, and then you can start putting it behind you."

"This is it then," Aaron said when he finally relented. "I'm never going to do anything else for him! Nothing! I'm going to see him, I'm leaving, and then I'm done with him."

Thomas nodded, and Aaron left to see Bonnet.

When Aaron entered the small, windowless room he found two chairs separated by a narrow, scarred oak table. He sat in the chair nearest the door and soon Bonnet entered and took the other. He seemed to have aged ten years since his last appearance in the courtroom. Gray shadows haunted his eyes . . . his once smooth chin was covered in a scruffy beard and looked too sharp . . . his shoulders were hunched and thin. Aaron was surprised by his appearance.

"They've sentenced me to die." Bonnet's voice trembled as he laced his fingers together and rested his arms on the table.

Aaron glared at him.

"I have a letter for the governor," Bonnet went on. "Would you be so kind as to make certain he receives it?" He slid a folded paper across the table to Aaron with a shaky hand. Aaron took the letter but said nothing and continued glowering at Bonnet.

"I heard Thomas was released," Bonnet ventured.

"No thanks to you!" Aaron growled through clenched teeth.

"Harriot made me do it!" Bonnet defended himself, and Aaron heard that weak, sniveling whine in his father's voice that he hated. "He said we could help Thomas better if we were free ourselves."

"You're lying!" Aaron yelled as he felt a sneer curl his lip. "You weren't trying to save Thomas! You were trying to save yourself! You were only keeping yourself out of trouble—just like you always do! If for just once you could have done what was right . . ."

He expected Bonnet to argue with him or try to justify what he had done, but instead, Bonnet dropped his eyes to the floor and his shoulders sagged even further.

"I know," Bonnet whispered. "If I could do it all over again, things would be different."

"But you can't, can you?" Aaron raged. "Do you know how many people are dead because of you? What Sam's parents are going through because of you?"

Aaron could tell by the look on Bonnet's face that he had no idea who Samuel was, and that just fueled his rage. He stood, overturning his chair, and pounded on the table.

"My mother *died* because of you!"

"I loved her!" Bonnet protested.

"So did I!" Aaron said, his voice cracking, and he fled the room.

Outside, Aaron leaned against the building, trembling, though he hugged himself as hard as he could. He was still gripping the letter and was tempted to rip it up, but after he'd calmed down a bit, he unfolded it and began reading.

In it, Bonnet told the governor that he had become a Christian and was sorry for everything he had done. He begged the governor for mercy and pleaded for his life, saying that he would cut off his arms and legs if allowed to live—all he needed was his tongue to praise the Lord and seek salvation. He said that the reputation of his family lay in the governor's hands, and he appealed to the governor's Christianity and sense of charity.

Aaron couldn't believe what he was reading. *The reputation of his family?* Was he serious? Did he honestly think anyone was going to believe what was in this letter?

It would have been nice to think that everything Bonnet had said in the letter was true. For months after his mother had died, Aaron had stayed with Bonnet and done as he had been told. He'd put himself and his friends in grave danger and exposed all of them to things that no one should have witnessed or been a part of.

Why?

Why had he not abandoned Bonnet? Why had he stayed with him for so long?

Aaron knew in his heart that it was because he had always held out hope that one day Bonnet would say the very words that were in this letter.

And the irony of it was, now that Bonnet had finally said them, Aaron couldn't make himself believe they were true.

Aaron made his way to the governor's and delivered the letter, glad to be rid of it.

That, he thought, will be the last thing I ever do for Bonnet.

That you, the said Stede Bonnet, *shall go from hence to the Place from whence you came, and from thence to the Place of Execution, where you shall be hanged by the Neck till you are dead. And the God of infinite Mercy be merciful to your Soul.*
—*Judge Nicholas Trott, 1718*

~ ~ ~

The Hanging

The boys seemed to drift apart in the days before Bonnet's execution. Aaron didn't tell Thomas and Jonathan about the letter, but they could tell that he was upset. They seemed unsure what to say to him, so most of the time they said nothing as they wandered the streets or walked on the beach.

Realizing they couldn't live forever on what little was left of their gold stash, they pondered jobs, but most conversations of future plans seemed strained. There was a gloom over them all, and Aaron knew it wouldn't pass until Bonnet's hanging had been carried out.

Still, he welcomed the lack of conversation and spent his days trying to work out in his mind how he felt about Bonnet. Should he be upset about losing Bonnet simply because the man was his father? Bonnet had certainly never been fatherly toward him. Bonnet was weak and cowardly, wicked and cruel.

Aaron should be glad to see him go.

But somehow the thought that Bonnet had always made his mother happy stayed at the forefront of Aaron's mind.

Thinking back to his days on Barbados, Aaron remembered how the sounds and smells that he awoke to each morning would indicate what the day would bring. If the cabin was filled with the aroma of roast meat and fresh bread and the sound of his mother humming or singing, he would know Bonnet was coming. She would work happily all day and then listen for the sound of his knock at the door. She would fling it open eagerly to find Bonnet, grandiosely dressed and bearing flowers—always bearing flowers.

Those flowers were placed in a vase on the table and remained there until morning. Then his mother would tie them together with thin twine, pound a nail into one of the ceiling beams, and hang the flowers to dry.

She never removed any of them.

By the time his mother had died, the beams were so full of dried flowers that the ceiling looked like a spring meadow.

The night before the execution, Aaron lay awake, thinking about the letter. Had Bonnet really meant what he'd said? And if so, was Thomas right? Would God really forgive Bonnet?

Aaron pulled out the Smiths' Bible and leafed through it, looking for answers. He tried praying, but the only thing that came to his mind was that *he* was to forgive Bonnet.

He considered obeying this nudging, but ultimately Aaron decided that whatever else might happen, he was never going to be able to forgive his father. It was Bonnet's fault that his mother was dead, that he was without a family. It was Bonnet who had murdered Samuel.

Aaron was secure in his knowledge that Bonnet had done too many things to ever earn forgiveness, yet even after he decided that he would not—*could* not—forgive his father, he struggled with his thoughts throughout the night.

The words from Bonnet's letter swam in his head, and the idea that he should forgive Bonnet would not leave his mind.

In the morning, Aaron rose early and dressed as quietly as he could in the dim light. Just as he opened the door, Thomas stirred.

"What are you doing?" Thomas whispered.

"There's something I need to do," Aaron replied quietly over his shoulder, rushing from the room before Thomas could question him further.

South Carolina in December offered scant opportunity to collect flowers, but Aaron eventually accumulated enough to compose a small bouquet. He tied it together and turned to race toward the waterfront.

A large crowd had already gathered at White Point by the time he arrived. Some of the onlookers were protesting the execution, hoping for a last-minute reprieve, while others were clearly anxious to view another hanging.

Aaron pushed his way through the mass of people until he reached the edge of the route that Bonnet would travel. He stood among the onlookers, clutching the flowers he had gathered and wondering exactly what he was going to do with them now that he had them. A young girl stood next to Aaron. She saw the flowers in his hand and smiled at him, but Aaron ignored her and looked away.

Eventually a murmur rose from the crowd and the procession came into view. Although the hands of the pirates who had already been hanged had been tied behind their backs, Aaron noticed that Bonnet's wrists were bound in front of him and he briefly wondered why as he watched Bonnet sway with the movement of the horse-drawn cart, hair askew, face contorted with terror. Aaron was certain that Bonnet had been crying; indeed an occasional sob would rack his body as he was transported closer to the gallows.

As he drew nearer, his wild red eyes spotted Aaron and held his gaze. He seemed to calm and his gaze softened. The little girl next to Aaron noticed that Bonnet and Aaron were looking at each other and she tugged on his sleeve.

"Do you want to see him hang?" she asked. Aaron didn't look away from Bonnet as he spoke.

"I want him to know that . . ."

Know what? That he ruined my life? That I care? That I hate him? That I'm glad he made my mother so happy? That I wish he

172

wasn't my father? The thoughts were darting about in Aaron's mind until only one remained. *That I forgive him.*

Aaron looked down at the flowers and then the girl. "I was going to give him these," he said.

"So why don't you?"

But Aaron couldn't move.

"Do you want me to do it?" she asked, seeing that Aaron was about to miss his opportunity. She reached tentatively for the bouquet. Aaron looked down at the flowers one last time and nodded before releasing them to her. As Bonnet pulled even with them, the girl rushed forward and thrust the bouquet into his manacled hands.

Startled, Bonnet looked down at the flowers and then back to Aaron. As the wagon passed by, his fearful demeanor vanished completely and a look appeared on his face that Aaron had seen only one other time . . . the morning he and Bonnet had sailed out of Barbados.

Up until that day—the day the two of them had left the island—grief from the loss of Aaron's mother had hung over them both like a heavy cloak in summer. But on that morning, when Aaron had looked up at Bonnet, fully expecting to see his own sadness reflected once again, he had instead seen his father scanning the new horizon with an almost childlike eagerness. As Bonnet had looked across the vast ocean of possibilities, Aaron had seen on his face the same emotion—the same look—that he was seeing now.

It was the look of hope.

Aaron remembered only two details of the actual hanging—the cries of the crowd as Bonnet was yanked off the cart, and the sight of Bonnet's hands, still clutching the flowers long after he was dead.

The Night before he was killed, he (Teach) sat up and drank till the Morning, with some of his own Men, and the Master of a Merchant-Man, and having had Intelligence of the two Sloops coming to attack him, as has been before observed; one of his Men asked him, in Case any Thing should happen to him in the Engagement of the Sloops, whether his Wife knew where he had buried his Money? He answered, that no Body but himself and the Devil, knew where it was, and the longest Liver should take all.
—Daniel Defoe

~ ~ ~

A Hot Sky

The confusion Aaron had felt before Bonnet's execution was magnified after it. He waffled between long periods of silence when he wanted nothing more than to be by himself and times when he needed to ramble. Thomas and Jonathan were priceless—leaving him alone when he needed it or listening when he wanted to try to explain to them how he was feeling or to tell stories of his mother and Bonnet. It was as if Bonnet had been his last link to his mother, and sometimes the need to remember as much as he could and share it with them was almost overwhelming.

He had just finished telling them about a hat that Bonnet had given to his mother when suddenly, before he could stop himself, he started telling them about the letter Bonnet had written to the governor and how he had claimed to be a Christian.

"Do you think it's true?" he asked them. "Do you think he really was saved at the end, or was he just saying that so they wouldn't execute him?"

"It doesn't matter what we think," Thomas said. "The truth will be the same no matter what we choose to believe."

"But . . . I want to know."

"I know you do," Thomas said, "but the only person's salvation you can ever be certain of is your own."

Aaron immediately squirmed. Once again, he wondered if Thomas was questioning his faith. He felt himself growing angry and was tempted to abruptly change the subject, but it wasn't Thomas' fault. Aaron had been the one to bring it up in the first place. And besides, he had one more question.

"Why would God create someone if He was just going to let them burn in Hell forever? If He's kind and merciful, how can He let that happen to someone? I don't understand how a loving God could do that."

"He *is* kind and merciful," Thomas answered, "but He's just and righteous, too."

Aaron looked at him, unconvinced.

"We aren't going to understand everything," Thomas went on. "That's why He said that He'd leave us with a peace that surpassed our own understanding. It's all right if you don't understand something, but don't let that make you doubt God."

"I never said I doubted Him," Aaron replied, painfully aware of how defensive he sounded and definitely ready to change the subject now.

"No," Thomas smiled, "you didn't say that you doubted Him."

"Do you want to hear about the time Bonnet's horse bucked him?"

"Yes!" Jonathan said, laughing already as Thomas nodded. Aaron threw himself into the next story. He wanted to think about what Thomas had said, but he wanted to do it later, when he could be by himself.

After only a few days Aaron's emotions began to approach what was apparently going to be as close to normal as they were going to get, and the boys began to discuss with one another the fact that they had the complete freedom to do whatever they wanted now, yet they had no plans. Jonathan and Thomas mentioned finding other jobs on a merchant ship, but Aaron immediately began obsessing about finding Hannah and Samuel Smith, and—to his surprise and delight—the brothers once again agreed to help him in his quest to try to set things right. The three had little money left, but Aaron was confident that the pirates had hidden treasure during their travels.

Now, he made up his mind that he was going to find it.

At Aaron's request, the boys gathered in their room, and Aaron pulled from beneath the bed the items that he had taken from Richards' body—the pistols, the knife, and the folded piece of paper. He passed a pistol to Thomas, he gave the knife to Jonathan, and then he spread the paper out before them all.

"I think Richards hid something," he said, "and I think this can tell us where it is."

The three boys leaned over the paper and studied it together. There were seemingly random letters scattered around with one name circled in the middle—Caroline Eure. After discussing several possibilities, Thomas wondered aloud if it could represent a graveyard.

"That's what I was thinking." Aaron nodded. "These initials here are to orient you in the graveyard"—he slid his finger over to another set—"then these here tell you which row and how far over. It must be buried in Caroline Eure's grave."

"It's buried in a *grave*?" Jonathan asked, his eyes bugging to the size of giant clams.

"Probably," Thomas said.

"But where?" Aaron asked.

"Ocracoke?" Thomas suggested.

"Maybe," Aaron agreed, but he sounded unconvinced. "We can't just hit every graveyard on the Eastern Coast until we find the right one. We've got to figure out a way to narrow it down."

They puzzled quietly for a few minutes about where Richards would have been most likely to hide treasure, and then suddenly, Jonathan broke the silence.

"A-hot-sky!" he said excitedly. Aaron and Thomas looked at each other and then back at Jonathan, confused.

"A-hot-sky!" Jonathan repeated, waving his hand crazily, obviously frustrated that they did not understand something that was so clear to him. "The night Israel Hands was shot—that's what he must have been talking about. Now it all makes sense!"

Aaron and Thomas plied Jonathan with questions and listened intently as the boy relayed the events of that evening to them—the evening after the three captains had returned from their mysterious absence so badly sunburned.

"Hands got really drunk that night," Jonathan began. "He kept talking about a funeral and I could tell that Blackbeard and Richards were getting angry with him for some reason. Richards left, but Blackbeard stayed. Then he shot Hands under the table."

"But Blackbeard said he did that to remind everyone who was in charge," Aaron said.

"No," Thomas countered. "Blackbeard said if he didn't *kill* one of them every now and then that they would forget who was in charge. But he *didn't* kill him—he only injured him. If Blackbeard had really meant to kill Hands, Hands would be dead."

They all agreed on this point.

"So why did he shoot him then?" Aaron asked slowly, trying to understand.

"Because Harriot, Bonnet, and I were there too," Jonathan continued. "Blackbeard didn't want anyone else to know about it and Hands wouldn't stop talking. He kept going on and on about it being the saddest funeral he'd ever been to—but he wasn't sad at all—he was laughing! Blackbeard knew that Bonnet and Harriot were going to figure out what he was talking about if he didn't shut him up—shooting him was the easiest way to make him stop talking." Jonathan puffed out his chest, obviously very pleased with himself for figuring all this out. "That's got to be it . . . A-hot-sky."

Thomas and Aaron looked at each other in amazement and repeated in unison, "A-hot-sky!"

Laughing, Thomas punched Jonathan on the arm, and Jonathan, grinning, punched Thomas back and burst out laughing. The punching and laughing continued until suddenly they both stopped and looked at Aaron.

Aaron stopped smiling and attempted to put a fearful look on his face.

"A-hot-sky?" he asked in a small voice, trying not to laugh.

They lunged at him, screaming like maniacs. All three bodies thudded to the floor, but the sound was drowned out by the laughter ringing through the air.

Hands *being taken, was try'd and condemned, but just as he was about to be executed, a Ship arrived at* Virginia *with a Proclamation for prolonging the Time of his Majesty's Pardon to such of the Pyrates as should surrender by a limited Time therein expressed: Notwithstanding the Sentence,* Hands *pleaded the Pardon, and was allowed the Benefit of it, and was alive some Time ago in* London, *begging his Bread.*
—Daniel Defoe

~ ~ ~

Caroline Eure

They were almost out of money. Anxious as they were to head back to Holiday Island to begin their search for Caroline Eure's grave, they needed money for room, board, and fare for boat passage to North Carolina. With their eyes on a goal, each of them found a job.

Jonathan worked for the owner of the inn they were staying at, doing whatever needed to be done. He cooked and swept and washed dishes. He didn't earn any money, but the owner agreed to let all three of them continue staying and eating there at no charge, so they were able to save all of Thomas' and Aaron's wages.

Thomas spent each day at the harbor and soon developed a reputation among the captains who sailed into and out of the port. If they needed additional help loading or unloading cargo, Thomas was usually chosen first among the men who were looking for work. He was strong and quick, but mostly he was wanted because he was a hard and dependable worker. While other men did the bare minimum they felt they could get away with, Thomas did as much as he possibly could, and at the end of each work day, he usually had two shillings to show for his work—sometimes three.

Aaron found steady employment with a local furniture maker, Mr. Davis. He spent most of his time alone, usually sanding or waxing the wood. Mr. Davis often tried to teach Aaron additional skills—how to join two pieces of wood

together, or how to measure spindles for a certain piece—
but Aaron politely made it clear that he wasn't going to be
staying long enough to make it worth the man's time.

"You'd be wise to start thinking on a profession now,
young man," Mr. Davis said one day, running his hand over
the back of a chair he'd just finished. "You'd do well to
consider staying here."

Aaron didn't want a job like this though, where there
was so little interaction with other people. He thought
about Sam's father and wondered what he did for a living.
Was it something that he would have trained Sam in? Did
they own a business? A farm? Sam had probably been old
enough to start helping his father in his work. His father
might have been depending on the extra hands. Maybe it
was something that *Aaron* would be able to help him
with . . . he'd have to wait and see.

"I can't stay much longer," Aaron told Mr. Davis for
what seemed like the hundredth time.

"I wish you'd change your mind," his employer said
somberly, pressing a Spanish dollar into Aaron's hand. Mr.
Davis took another dollar and, with his knife, broke it into
fourths. He gave Aaron one of the pieces—a full reale
more than he usually made in a week.

"Thank you," Aaron said.

Mr. Davis smiled and Aaron saw true kindness and
concern in his eyes. "You're a good worker. I hope you'll
be back."

Aaron nodded. He'd be back. He wouldn't leave
without saying goodbye, and they didn't have enough
money just yet for boat fare anyway.

They were close though. It wouldn't be much longer.

Three weeks later the boys sat on the floor of their
room, counting their money. It was a conglomeration of
coins from different countries and was difficult to add up,
but Thomas finally declared that they had enough to head
to North Carolina. Aaron put in one more full day with Mr.

Davis and then broke it to him that he wouldn't be returning. When he got back to the room, Thomas and Jonathan had packed what few things they owned. Eager to start their new adventure, the boys willingly went to sleep early that night, as their ship would be sailing just after first light.

Only a few days later, shielding their eyes from the midday sun, the boys stood among a throng of passengers lined up along the rail of their ship. As it bobbed gently in the shallow sound, they gazed with wide eyes at the shoreline of North Carolina. The landscape was flat and unremarkable, but Aaron knew from their previous visit that the forests were dense and hid hushed secrets.

"There's Ocracoke," they heard the captain say.

"Isn't that where Blackbeard was taken?" a man asked.

"Indeed it is," the captain nodded.

The boys exchanged hasty glances, and Thomas approached the captain.

"Excuse me," Thomas said, "but what did you just say about Blackbeard?"

"Haven't you heard? The most notorious pirate of all times was finally brought down," he jabbed his thumb in the direction of the shoreline, "right there."

All three of the boys sucked in a breath.

"What happened to him?" Thomas asked.

"He lost his head's what happened to him!" a man interjected.

The captain nodded. "A bloody battle they say it was. Lieutenant Maynard cut his head off, tied it onto the bow of his boat, and threw his body into the sea."

"What about his crew?" Aaron wanted to know, immediately worried about Husk.

"They're all gone."

"Surely not all of them were killed?"

"Some of them were killed during the battle, the rest were hanged after their trial—well, all except for a few who were pardoned."

"Pardoned?" Aaron breathed hopefully. "Who was pardoned?"

"I don't know their names. One of them had just been captured a day or two before and was able to prove he wasn't one of them. Another one turned king's evidence . . . the rest were hanged last week in Virginia."

Maybe it was Husk. Maybe Husk had turned king's evidence.

The captain walked away. As soon as he was gone, Jonathan whispered to Thomas.

"What if it was Hands? What if Israel Hands is the one who turned king's evidence?"

"Or what if Hands told whoever it was where the treasure is?" Aaron said.

"Do you want to quit looking?" Thomas asked them.

They both shook their heads.

"The only thing for us to do is to keep going and to hope that whoever was pardoned doesn't know about the treasure."

"Or," Jonathan said, staring at the shore, "hope that we get there first."

Aaron started to worry. Not only was there now the possibility that someone else might get to the treasure before them, but he wasn't even sure that they would be able to find it. All they had was a crude map of what they *thought* was a graveyard probably located somewhere near Holiday Island. Considering that the pirates had traveled up and down the length of the Atlantic, they had certainly narrowed it down, but they truly had no idea where to look once they arrived.

"How are we going to find 'A-Hot-Sky'?" Aaron asked Thomas.

"Are you just now wondering about that?"

182

Aaron nodded.

"I've already thought about it a lot," Thomas said. Somehow Aaron wasn't surprised. "Come on," Thomas said. "I'll show you."

They went to the captain's quarters and knocked. The captain answered the door and let them in.

"Sorry to bother you," Thomas said.

"No problem at all," the captain replied. "You wish to see the map again?"

"Yes, please," Thomas said, "if you don't mind."

The captain spread a map of the coast of North Carolina out on his table and left them alone.

"This is the Cape Fear River, where our camp was." Thomas was tapping the map. He moved his finger north. "Here's Beaufort, you remember where that was."

Let's see . . . Oh yes, the place where you and Jonathan decided to give up your freedom so that you could follow me about and almost get yourself executed . . .

"I remember."

"Holiday Island is up here," Thomas slid his finger directly north of Bath.

"All right," Aaron said. He didn't have any idea how Thomas knew this but didn't doubt him for a second. Thomas grinned, probably at the clueless look on Aaron's face. It was pretty clear that he might as well be talking about Easter Island as far as Aaron's bearings were concerned.

"It's right up this river," Thomas explained. "The Chowan River. When the men came back that night, they returned from the east, so 'A-Hot-Sky' must be over here."

"That's still a pretty big area," Aaron said. The map showed nothing but land stretching east of the river. If it was anything like the land that they'd seen from the river, then it was swampy and overgrown and uninhabited.

"It is," Thomas agreed, "but I think we can narrow it down."

"How?"

"We'll stop at this lighterage port, here," he said, sliding his finger slightly south. "Someone will probably have a more detailed map of the land to look at. We can ask around. Even if there's not a map, someone will probably know what we're talking about."

"Yes," Aaron said. "We'll just ask them where we can find 'Roy-hot-skue' or 'Ar-hu-sky' or something that sounds like 'A-Hot-Sky.' I'm certain someone will be able to help us right out!"

Jonathan picked that moment to poke his head into the cabin.

"It's time to eat!" he said as Thomas and Aaron burst into laughter. "What's so funny?"

"We're just glad to see you!" Aaron said.

"And glad it's time to eat," Thomas added.

Jonathan looked confused but turned around and led them down the corridor and up the steps to the deck.

Thomas' plan worked quite well. When they reached the lighterage port of Portsmouth, they were able to locate a more detailed map at a shipping company. On this map, a few miles east of Holiday Island, they found a town that someone had labeled as "Ahoskie," and they immediately agreed that this was likely their "A-Hot-Sky." They began their search just west of Ahoskie and only had to eliminate two graveyards before they found the one that appeared to be what they were looking for.

Aaron went to one corner and called out, "William T. Vanhoy," while Thomas looked for the initials WTV on the paper. To their shock, the initials matched. Jonathan ran to a second corner and found a match for JSF with Jonathan Samuel Faison.

Excitement raced through Aaron's veins. *Could this really be happening?*

At Thomas' insistence, he and Jonathan checked the other two corners as well. Sure enough, the map was playing out. Pulse racing, his breathing fast and shallow,

Aaron walked with his friends as they searched for the elusive Caroline Eure.

It only took a few moments to find her grave and the boys stood above it once they had, staring at it in disbelief.

"I can't believe we've found it," Aaron whispered in awe.

"What do we do now?" Jonathan asked, dread thickening his voice.

Thomas suggested that they needed to dig at night to avoid detection and they agreed that they would return at dusk with tools and bags.

The boys came back just as darkness was settling its shadowy tentacles around the graveyard. With his back to the grave, Jonathan stood watch, holding a lamp up high, while Thomas and Aaron, intent on their task, began stabbing shovels into the cold, frost-covered ground.

Aaron's fingers soon cramped from the biting air, making it more difficult to clutch the tool. "How deep do you think we'll have to dig?" he asked.

Thomas blew warm breath into his cupped hands. "I'm not certain."

The work was heavy and before long sweat chased any thoughts of the cold away. Under the frost was a world of living creatures tunneling and crawling, trying to escape the assault from above.

"Here's something for you, Jonathan," Thomas said, holding out a cupped hand.

"What is it?" Jonathan asked, extending his open palm.

Thomas dropped something into Jonathan's hand and Jonathan held the lantern to it, gasping and throwing it quickly back at Thomas. Aaron looked down. It was a shiny white grub, wriggling frantically in the dim lantern light.

"That's mean!" Jonathan whispered harshly as Thomas and Aaron snickered.

"I hate it here. I wish you'd hurry up."

"I think we're almost there," Aaron said.

"Really?"

"I think I heard something though . . . listen."

All three stopped moving and stood quietly.

"Listen," Aaron said again, pointing to the hole. "Do you hear that?"

Jonathan leaned in and Thomas reached up and grabbed him, pulling him into the hole.

Jonathan screamed so loud that Aaron was afraid everyone for miles around would hear. He and Thomas howled with laughter and could hardly catch their breath.

"Oh, you're both REAL FUNNY!" Jonathan said, scrambling out of the hole. Thomas and Aaron laughed harder as Jonathan stalked off with the lantern and suddenly they were left in the darkness. Thomas hoisted himself out of the hole and chased after the glow of the lantern that was bobbing away.

"We're sorry," Thomas said, still laughing.

"You sound truly sorry," Jonathan said.

"Come on back, Jonathan," Aaron called, trying not to laugh. "We won't do it anymore."

"Come back. We're sorry," Thomas said, the laughter still in his voice.

"It's not funny!"

"I know ... I know it's not funny. See? I'm not laughing anymore."

Jonathan held the lantern toward Thomas' face.

"You are too."

Aaron burst into fresh laughter.

"And so is he!" Jonathan said, swinging the lantern in Aaron's direction.

"All right, all right," Thomas said. "We'll stop. We'll stop—won't we, Aaron?"

"Yes," Aaron said, trying to compose himself.

Grudgingly, Jonathan finally returned to the grave and held the lantern over it. For the next hour Thomas and Aaron stifled occasional laughs and Jonathan refused to talk to either one of them. Eventually, though, fatigue got the better of them all and they fell to working in silence.

Jonathan was stretching and yawning, causing the lamp to throw crazy shadows everywhere, when Thomas' spade finally hit the top of the coffin. The boys dug with new fervor, then swept the rest of the dirt away with their hands. Like starving monkeys, they tugged and pulled at the coffin's lid. Damp and rotten, it broke easily as they pried off pieces and tossed them over their shoulders. Jonathan swung the lantern more directly over the hole and they all peered in. Dirt and sediment had seeped into the coffin, filling it almost to the top, yet they could see bits of gold, glimmering through the debris in the dim lantern light.

Thomas and Aaron used their hands to sift through the dirt and pull out the treasure. Jonathan lowered the lantern to give them more light and watched with a grimace. He was clearly appalled at what they were doing but, at the same time, so astonished at what they were finding that he apparently could not turn away. There were some copper and brass coins, but most of the money was silver (reales, shillings, crowns, groats, and livres) or gold (guineas, doubloons, pistoles, and escudos). Some of the coins they had never seen before or didn't recognize but they threw them into the bags with just as much glee as the rest.

In addition to coins, they discovered ivory carved with intricate designs, strands of pearls, and silver buckles. They found seven emeralds, dozens of rubies, and a small bag of diamonds. More than once they came across leather pouches filled with gold dust that were still intact, but most of the treasure had apparently been thrown in loose on top of the body or buried in cloth sacks that had long since disintegrated. As they got closer to the bottom of the coffin, Aaron and Thomas had to pick through rags and bones as well as dirt, sometimes reaching into the collapsed ribcage of Caroline Eure to salvage smaller items.

When they had neared the end and had filled so many bags that Aaron briefly worried how they were going to lug them all away, he spotted a gold ring. Reaching for it, he discovered that it was still around one of the skeleton's fingers. He started to slip it off, but Thomas touched his hand.

"Don't," Thomas said, looking at the ring.

"Why not?

"That's not ours," he said gently, and Aaron realized that Thomas was right.

Painstakingly they filled the grave back in and replaced the dirt and headstone with great care. Daylight was threatening to set fire to the horizon as they stepped back and looked at the grave of Caroline Eure. They stood in silence for a long moment, then quietly picked up their bags of riches and headed toward the sunrise.

It was as they reached the edge of the graveyard that they heard a noise that caused Jonathan to lift the lantern toward the woods. They were astounded to see the barrel of a pistol slide out of the shadows, held by a limping and ragged Israel Hands.

He ordered them to drop everything and they all did—even Jonathan, who threw the lantern down.

The lantern immediately flickered out, but there was enough light from the approaching sun for Aaron to realize that Israel Hands was a skeleton of his former self. Dirty and emaciated, his clothes hung from him in rags. Had he been out in the woods this whole time, Aaron wondered, perhaps searching for the treasure?

Even with the drop on them, Aaron felt that Hands wasn't that intimidating, and apparently Thomas thought so, too. His hands halfway raised out of instinct, Aaron glanced at Thomas and realized that he was drawing his pistol. Instantly, Aaron did the same and Jonathan drew his knife, only a split second behind the older boys.

Hands' eyes bulged and suddenly he turned to flee, hobbling into the forest. Thomas chased after him, quickly tackling him and wrenching the pistol from his hands. Aaron was standing over them both, pointing his own pistol at Hands' head.

The feeble pirate started trembling and weeping, begging for his life. Thomas tossed Hands' pistol to Jonathan and then cautiously searched the pirate for more weapons. When he was convinced that Hands was no longer armed, Thomas got up and stepped back, aiming his own gun as well.

"What are you going to do to me?" Hands cried, looking at the three pistols that were trained on him.

"Who's with you?" Thomas wanted to know.

"No one's with me—I've come alone."

They all peered past him into the woods, now brightening with morning rays.

"There's no one left, remember?" Aaron realized, looking at Thomas. "Just him." He turned back to Hands. "You testified against them, didn't you?"

Hands nodded.

"Is Husk dead?" Aaron asked.

Hands nodded again.

"Was he killed in the battle or did they hang him?" For some reason, Aaron needed to know.

"Battle," Hands answered so softly that Aaron could barely hear him. Aaron felt surprisingly relieved. There had been enough hangings. Husk had died on the ship—at sea—where he belonged.

"Get out of here!" Thomas ordered, kicking dirt at the pitiful man.

Confusion and then relief swept over Hands' face as he realized that Thomas meant to let him go. He struggled to his feet and turned quickly, limping into the deep shadows of the woods.

Aaron watched Hands go, forcing himself to put it from his mind that Husk was dead. They had the treasure now. Aaron was going to find the Smiths and then everything was going to be all right. He was only going to allow himself to concentrate on the bright future.

When they were certain that Hands was gone, the boys slowly lowered their pistols and exchanged nervous glances. Finally Aaron said to Thomas, "Mine wasn't even loaded—was yours?"

"No," Thomas said sheepishly.

"Oh, don't worry," Jonathan assured them, holding up his knife. "Mine was!" and the three of them dissolved into laughter.

If there were a yearly supply of ten or a dozen such missionaries sent abroad into their respective countries, after they had received the degree of master of arts in the aforesaid college, and holy orders in England, (till such time as episcopacy be established in those parts) it is hardly to be doubted, but, in a little time the world would see good and great effects thereof.
—*A Proposal For the Better Supplying of Churches in our Foreign Plantations and for Converting the Savage Americans to Christianity*

~ ~ ~

Grace Church

The long trip from the coast of North Carolina to Nassau Island in New York gave Aaron plenty of chances to rehearse what he was going to say when he finally found the Smiths.

Don't be afraid. I'm here to make things right. My father was the one who killed your son, but I'm so very sorry for what he did.

I know this won't bring your son back, but I want to give you this. He would thrust a large bag of gold toward them. *To make things easier for you. I know how awful you must feel.*

Of course they would be overwhelmed, and then they would tell Aaron that he was not responsible for what his father had done and try to refuse the money. But Aaron would insist. He would tell them that he knew what it was like to lose someone you love . . . he would tell them about his mother.

Sometimes in his daydreams they would feel very sorry for him and invite him in.

Sometimes he envisioned himself convincing Samuel to let him work with him. He pictured himself working side by side with Samuel, doing the jobs that had been intended for Sam. They might be reluctant at first, but after they got to know him . . .

And sometimes he let himself fanaticize that they might actually welcome him into their lives, that they would tell him he could stay. They would be his family and he wouldn't be alone anymore . . .

He relished this daydream most of all, and although he tried to stop it, his mind wandered to it every day. But even when he allowed himself the luxury of these thoughts, he never let them get too far out of hand. He wouldn't call them his mother and father, and he knew that he would never replace their son. But was there really any reason that they couldn't fill a void in each other's lives? Couldn't they help one another get through what Bonnet had done to them? Wouldn't it be a good thing if they came to care for one other?

Aaron dared to let himself believe that it might happen just that way.

He tried to tell himself that giving them the money and apologizing for what Bonnet had done was going to be enough. He knew that they may want him to go away—that seeing his face every day might be too hurtful of a reminder of what had happened—but he found himself actually daring to ask God for a family, and his fantasy grew daily.

Speaking of God . . .

He had continued thinking on the things Thomas had spoken with him about. He had been reading Hannah Smith's Bible. He decided that Christ's sacrifice was great enough to forgive even the most horrendous of crimes. If God could forgive Bonnet, shouldn't Aaron, too?

Judge not, and ye shall not be judged. Condemn not, and ye shall not be condemned. Forgive, and ye shall be forgiven.

Aaron wanted that forgiveness. He wasn't the monster his father had been, but he knew that *any* sin was enough to separate him from God . . . and he didn't want to be separated. He was thankful he had given the flowers to Bonnet and thankful for the forgiveness he'd been able to muster up. He was thankful for the forgiveness that continued to grow inside of him even now.

By the time Nassau Island appeared on the horizon, Aaron had begun to share with Thomas and Jonathan bits and pieces of what he hoped might happen when he found the Smiths. They exchanged uneasy glances, and finally Thomas suggested that perhaps Aaron was getting his hopes up, but Aaron would hear none of it.

"You just don't want me to be happy!" he snapped at Thomas. Of course he knew this wasn't true, but the daydreams he had developed of a life with Samuel and Hannah were so pleasant that he couldn't stand any talk that threatened to smother them. Starting a disagreement was a senseless thing to do, but it succeeded in squelching Thomas' warnings. Thomas didn't say another word until they disembarked the ship, and when he finally did speak again, it was with a resigned effort to be supportive.

"What would you like to do now?" Thomas asked him, clutching the one small bag he'd brought with him from North Carolina.

"Find a room and start looking for Grace Church."

"Fine," Thomas agreed. There was only a slight edge to his voice, but Aaron did not miss it.

They looked for a room for the night, but every place they tried was full. Finally they stood outside a posh-looking inn just as the sun set. Massive white columns rose toward the sky, the elegant red-brick building was adorned with perfectly manicured greenery, and slaves wearing the whitest stockings Aaron had ever seen assisted weary travelers down from coaches.

"I guess we'd better try here," Thomas said, admiring the inn from the curb.

"It looks expensive," Aaron said.

"Well, it's not as if we don't have plenty of money," Thomas reminded him, and Aaron nodded.

They had divided the treasure into four equal shares— one for each of them and one for the Smiths. Money wasn't going to be a problem for any of them for a long time to come.

They entered the inn and inquired about a room. A beanpole of a man with a very sharp nose and thin, black hair looked over his spectacles at the boys. "We've nothing available."

"Why are there no rooms anywhere?" Aaron asked, exasperated.

"Horse racing at the Round House," the clerk explained. "Everyone who's anyone wants to be at Newmarket tomorrow."

"How much?" Thomas asked, ignoring the horse racing handbill the clerk was pointing to.

"I've told you . . . we've nothing available."

"How much?" Thomas asked again.

The clerk paused for a moment, looking at each of them before replying quietly, "You don't have enough."

Thomas placed a leather pouch on the counter, the coins inside jingling unmistakably. A quick look of surprise crossed the clerk's face.

"Ten pounds," he finally said.

Aaron sucked in his breath. Ten pounds was three months' salary. Thomas didn't hesitate. He pulled out three guineas and slid them across the counter.

"*Each*," the clerk said.

Thomas slid six more gold coins toward him.

With a look of astonishment, the clerk collected the coins and showed them to a room.

"How'd you know he had a room, Thomas?" Jonathan asked after they closed the door.

"Look at us," Thomas said. Aaron looked at Thomas and Jonathan and then at himself in the mirror. Their clothes were threadbare in spots and ill-fitting. Dirt was packed under their fingernails and their hair was tangled and filthy. Most likely, they didn't smell like roses, either.

"He just didn't want us staying here and probably thought we couldn't afford it anyway. He figured if he set the price high enough we'd leave."

"I think we need to buy some new clothes," Aaron suggested, speaking more to Jonathan than Thomas.

194

"And baths," Jonathan said. Thomas nodded in agreement, but it was obvious he still hadn't forgotten their earlier row.

Later, alone in the bathhouse, Aaron examined his scars as he dried off. They had faded since that night so long ago, but they were still quite visible and he knew they would always be there—a constant reminder of his days on the *Revenge* . . .

A constant reminder of Pell.

He thought of how he had finally managed to forgive his father, and he wondered now if he would ever be able to forgive Pell in the same way. It was what God wanted from him. He knew that. He gently ran a finger along the scar on his chest. He swallowed hard and closed his eyes.

He wanted to do what was right.

But I can't do it on my own, he prayed. *You're going to have to help me.*

And when he opened his eyes, he had no doubt that God was going to do just that.

Aaron was too tense to eat any dinner and he went to bed early that night. Although he was excited to be so close to finding the Smiths, he was also upset about the way he had spoken to Thomas that afternoon. He lay in bed for a long time, unable to get to sleep. Finally he sat up and looked at Thomas.

"Thomas," he said. "I'm sorry. I shouldn't have gotten mad at you earlier."

"That's all right," Thomas said, and Aaron knew that he meant it. "I just don't want you to get hurt."

"I'm not going to get hurt," Aaron assured him. "I know what I'm doing."

"I hope so."

Aaron heard the doubt in his voice, but he ignored it. He was certain that tomorrow he was finally going to be a part of a real family.

Happy and content, he lay back down and finally went to sleep.

The next morning, despite the fact that his stomach was empty from not having eaten any dinner the night before, Aaron didn't go to breakfast with Jonathan and Thomas. He was too nervous right now. As soon as he found the Smiths he would calm down, and he could eat then.

He dressed in his new clothes and stood assessing himself in front of the mirror. His hair—washed, brushed, and tied back with a silk ribbon—was lighter and his body was taller, darker, and broader than when he'd left Barbados. He had been a boy when they'd set sail almost two years ago, but now a young man was staring back at him.

Aaron looked out the window at the street below him, lined with large oaks and filled with the flow of wagons and people, and then to the clean, brick buildings beyond. He smiled at the thought of the family God was about to give him. He wondered what Hannah and Samuel were doing right now. He imagined, for what seemed like the thousandth time, the looks on their faces when they invited him into their lives. Thomas and Jonathan entered the room, interrupting his daydream.

"I'm ready," Aaron announced, turning around to face them.

"Do you want us to go with you?" Thomas asked.

Aaron thought for a moment. "Maybe to help me find them," he said, "but I think I should talk to them by myself."

Thomas nodded and the three set off to search for the Smiths.

"How do we find them?" Thomas asked as they stepped out of the building.

"First we have to find Grace Church and talk to the minister. He'll know where they are."

They hadn't walked too far when the streets grew crowded.

"Excuse me, sir," Aaron asked a well-dressed man. "Could you please tell us how to find Grace Church?"

The gentleman shook his head. "No indeed. I'm not from the island."

Next they approached a man and woman walking arm in arm.

"Pardon me," Thomas asked. "Could you give us directions to Grace Church?"

"I'm sorry," was the reply. "We're from out of town."

"All these people . . . doesn't anybody *live* here?" Jonathan asked after two more tries.

"I'll bet they're all here for the horse races," Thomas said, as Aaron asked another man.

"Grace Church," the man said, leading them a brief way down the street, "is that way." Pointing and gesticulating, he directed them to the church. "It's a small, square building . . . made of stone."

"Thank you," Aaron said, and they set off in the direction the man had indicated.

Once they reached the church, they entered and found an older man distributing hymnals to the pews.

"Reverend Poyer?" Aaron asked.

"I'm afraid you have the wrong Reverend," the older man said, pausing in his work. "Three different congregations meet here. It confuses many people. Reverend Poyer leads *Grace* Church."

"Can you tell us where to find him?"

"Certainly. He lives not far from here," the Reverend said, giving them directions. They set off down the street and quickly found the correct house. Holding the Smiths' Bible in one hand and clasping Hannah's cross in the other, Aaron rapped on the door. Reverend Poyer, a young man with a friendly smile and hair the color of cornsilk, answered the door.

"May I help you, young man?"

"Yes, sir," Aaron said. "I am looking for a family from your congregation and was hoping you could help me find them. Their name is Smith—Samuel and Hannah Smith."

Confusion flickered briefly across his face, but then the Reverend quickly composed himself and with a sweeping gesture of his hand offered, "Won't you please come in?"

"Thank you," Aaron said. Thomas and Jonathan followed Aaron into the parlor as they all took a seat.

"May I ask why you are looking for the Smiths?"

"I have some things that belong to them," Aaron said, holding out the Bible. The Reverend took the Bible from Aaron's hand and leafed through the first few pages, stopping on the record of baptism. He smiled, looked up at Aaron, and then handed the Bible back to him.

"Young Sam was the first person I baptized as Reverend of this congregation."

Aaron swallowed hard.

"Where did you get their Bible?"

"It was stolen from them. I . . . I wanted to return it." He held up the cross. "I have this too," he said, and then he pulled out a bag of money and set it down on the small table in front of him. "And this."

Reverend Poyer looked at the cross and then at the bag. He leaned forward, pulled apart the drawstrings, and peered into the bag.

"This wasn't stolen from them," he said, unable to hide his surprise. "Where did it come from?"

"It's for them."

"But this doesn't belong to Hannah and Samuel. They would *never* have had this much money."

"I . . . I wanted them to have it."

"Why?"

"Because of . . . because of what happened."

"Something has happened?"

Aaron swallowed hard a second time, fighting a lump in his throat.

"I don't understand why you want them to have this," the Reverend said, indicating the bag of money. "What is it that's happened?"

Aaron hadn't anticipated having to explain things to a stranger. Was it possible Reverend Poyer didn't know that Sam was dead? None of this was going the way he had planned. He gripped the Bible and cross tightly. If he could just talk to Hannah and Samuel, he knew they would understand exactly what he was trying to do.

"Can you please tell me where they are?"

"I wish I could," Reverend Poyer said, cinching the drawstrings to the bag shut and sliding it across the table toward Aaron.

"What do you mean?"

"I would have no way of knowing where to find them."

"Didn't they come home?"

"You mean here?"

Aaron nodded.

"This isn't their home."

"Where's their home?" Aaron asked, a feeling of panic rising in his throat.

"Hannah and Samuel live among whomever they're ministering to."

"I don't understand," Aaron said.

"Why . . . why Hannah and Samuel are missionaries—I assumed you knew."

Aaron shook his head.

"I thought they lived here," he said. "Sam was baptized here . . ."

Reverend Poyer nodded. "Indeed, Hannah and Samuel did come here periodically. They've been ministering to the natives of this land for almost ten years, but the last time I saw them they indicated they might be called to serve in the West Indies . . ."

"When was that?" Aaron asked, barely keeping the frustration from his voice.

"It must have been over a year ago . . ."

The panic that had been rising in his throat now shuddered throughout his body. This couldn't be right.

Aaron had been so certain—*so sure*—that he was going to have a family again that he could barely bring himself to believe that it *wasn't* going to happen. He needed to be alone . . . to think . . . to figure it all out.

Suddenly, strangely detached from everything around him, Aaron stood up.

"Thank you," he said, barely aware that he was talking.

"I'm very sorry young man," Reverend Poyer said as Aaron turned to leave. "Wait! Don't forget this . . ."

Aaron heard the coins jingle as the Reverend picked up the bag of money, but he kept walking.

"It's a donation," Aaron said, barely loud enough to be heard. "It's a donation to the church." He reached the door and pushed it open. Striding toward the street, Aaron was only vaguely aware that Thomas and Jonathan were close behind.

They walked in silence for some time, Aaron barely conscious of the clip-clop of horses and the ever-flowing crowd of people.

"I'm very sorry, Aaron," Thomas finally said. His voice sounded distant and muffled, as if unable to prevail against the thoughts in Aaron's head. Aaron kept walking.

Smoldering fire . . . calling for his mother . . . strong hands holding him back.

They turned a corner and Aaron's pace quickened. His pulse was pounding loudly in his ears.

"What are you going to do?" Jonathan asked.

"I'm going back to the room." Even his own voice scarcely penetrated his thoughts. They walked briskly through the growing crowd outside of the Round House. Aaron dodged past one person after another, barely aware of their presence.

Pell holding him . . . hurting him . . . bright red feathers fluttering to the floor.

Thomas' and Jonathan's footsteps quickened to keep up. The crowds were thinning. They were drawing close to

200

the inn. Was his hand bleeding? Surely it must be. He was gripping the cross so tightly . . .

Sam crumpling at his feet . . . Hannah reaching for her son . . . imploring Aaron to help.

He opened the door to the room and crossed to the window. People walked past on the street, vaporous and unclear. Everyone was going about their normal lives— walking . . . chatting . . . smiling. A slight breeze crossed his face.

Husk sailing away with Blackbeard . . . Bayley swinging from the gallows . . . Bonnet clutching a bouquet of flowers.

Aaron heard the door close and then muffled voices. He turned around in a foggy haze, standing by the window on legs that were about to collapse . . . Jonathan and Thomas were talking to him.

Suddenly Aaron's body heaved, trying to throw up, but his stomach was empty and dry. He sank to the floor as sobs racked his body and he drew his legs toward his chest, wrapping his arms around them.

Sobbing, he dropped his head onto his knees. His body rocked back and forth as if trying to rid himself of the pain.

"All I wanted was a family," he said desperately. "Why can't I have a family?"

Jonathan was crying too, on the floor, reaching for Aaron, trying to comfort him.

Only Thomas didn't cry.

He walked to Aaron and knelt down next to him, speaking quietly.

"We're brothers," he said.

"I know you are!" Aaron said angrily, drawing his knees in tighter. Why would Thomas say the one thing to him that could only hurt him more? Why would he remind Aaron that *they* had each other? That *they* were a family?

And instantly Aaron realized that he wouldn't.

Thomas would never say or do anything to hurt him.

"No," Thomas said, laying a hand on his arm. Aaron lifted his head to face him.

Laughter in a crowded tavern . . . a bell ringing on a shell-littered beach . . . cool water splashing on a hot summer's day . . .
He heard Thomas repeat it softly. "*We're* brothers."

And let us not be weary in well doing: for in due season we shall reap, if we faint not.
—Galatians 6:9

~ ~ ~
Epilogue

We know several things about what happened to Thomas, Jonathan, and Aaron after they traveled to Long Island (then called Nassau Island) to look for Hannah and Samuel Smith.

Aaron became a minister. He drew from his days on the *Revenge* extensively in his sermons and recorded many events in his journals. It is through his writings that we now have a clearer picture of the life of Stede Bonnet.

Thomas became a missionary and worked primarily with Spanish-speaking natives in the West Indies.

It is not clear what Jonathan did for much of his young adulthood, but we do know that eventually he settled in Rhode Island and was active in government.

And we know that they all stayed close.

We know that Aaron presided over the baptisms of Thomas' three daughters.

We know that he officiated at Jonathan's wedding ceremony and that he later baptized Jonathan's son.

And we know that Aaron named his firstborn son after his two best friends.

When Perry Newman found Reverend Aaron Lee's sermons and journals in the trunk that hot August day in 1965 and discovered that he was actually a descendant of Stede Bonnet, the Gentleman Pirate, he could scarcely believe that he had pirate blood coursing through his veins. He was so inspired, that—when I was born three months later—he insisted on naming me Leeann Elizabeth, after Aaron's mother, Ann Elizabeth Lee. Fortunately, my brother Patrick was born *before* the discovery. If not for that stroke of luck, I feel certain he would have gone through life bearing the unfortunate name of Stede Bonnet.

Dad loved to tell the story at cocktail parties and tried to impress anyone who would listen with details of the lives of his famous ancestor ("Actually worked side by side with Blackbeard—*Blackbeard*, I tell you!") until I am quite certain people cringed when they saw him coming. My brother and I were forced to dress as pirates at Halloween every year until we were old enough to convincingly express our desires to wear something else.

Even golf games were turned into an opportunity to brag about his claim to fame. "Ahoy, Matey" replaced "Fore" as he shielded his eyes from the sun to watch his ball sail toward the green.

Of course, Dad was not the only one who enjoyed boasting about our family history. I too would share the story from time to time (although not with the flair and gusto that my father managed to interject into every telling).

It was my husband's cousin, Betsy, who encouraged me to put the story down in writing. I was initially reluctant for several reasons. First of all, I write contemporary Christian fiction—not historical fiction—and I was confident I did not have what it would take to do this historical story justice. (Fortunately, God put the wonderful author Heather Frey Blanton in my path to take care of that concern!) Furthermore, I doubted my ability to conduct the research necessary to complete the story (history is truly *not* my strength!).

But mostly I worried that Aaron's version of events would not corroborate what I found.

What if history contradicted the stories that Dad and I had so loved to share?

I was both relieved and excited to find not only that history supported Aaron's account of the life of Stede Bonnet, but in fact that the details of the events provided by Aaron's writings shed light on many historical facts and answered many questions that—until now—one could only guess at.

On November 21, 1996, Mike Daniel and his dive team discovered a shipwreck in the shallow waters of Beaufort Inlet (formerly known as Topsail Inlet). A large team of scientists from a variety of educational, historical, and maritime institutions have been recovering and studying artifacts from the shipwreck site since that time, and all evidence supports the theory that the *Queen Anne's Revenge* has indeed been found. A large platter, pewterware, a pewter syringe, a hand grenade, lead shot, cannons, and gold are just some of the many items recovered. It is quite likely that many of the artifacts being found today were once seen and touched by my great-great-great-great-great-great-great-great-great-great-great-grandfather!

One of the finds is a bell that is dated 1705. I had the honor of seeing that bell on exhibit at the North Carolina Maritime Museum in Beaufort.

I think of the bell that the boys found that day on the beach in the Bahamas and I imagine them, playing like my son and his friends did as they were growing up.

In my mind, Aaron, Thomas, and Jonathan are nothing more than three boys, playing tag on the beach.

They splash through the surf and jump over driftwood.

They chase each other, darting and laughing . . . I can taste the salted air.

I see them running along the sand toward the bell.

One of them picks it up and swings it.

I hear it peal.

I feel it ringing in my bones.

~The End~

The hanging of Stede Bonnet, December 10th, 1718
at White Point in Charleston, South Carolina.

NEAR THIS SPOT IN THE AUTUMN OF 1718,
STEDE BONNET, NOTORIOUS "GENTLEMAN
PIRATE," AND TWENTY NINE OF HIS MEN,
CAPTURED BY COLONEL WILLIAM RHETT,
MET THEIR JUST DESERTS AFTER A TRIAL
AND CHARGE, FAMOUS IN AMERICAN HISTORY,
BY CHIEF JUSTICE NICHOLAS TROTT.
LATER NINETEEN OF RICHARD WORLEY'S CREW,
CAPTURED BY GOVERNOR ROBERT JOHNSON,
WERE ALSO FOUND GUILTY AND HANGED.
ALL WERE BURIED OFF WHITE POINT GARDENS,
IN THE MARSH BEYOND LOW-WATER MARK

Photograph of the marker used to commemorate the trial and hanging of Stede Bonnet and his men. The marker is located in White Point Gardens, Charleston, South Carolina, on South Battery, between East Battery and Church Street.

The bell, and other artifacts from the *Queen Anne's Revenge* excavation site, on display at the North Carolina Maritime Museum in Beaufort.

The author, holding a piece of concretion from Blackbeard's *Queen Anne's Revenge* at the Underwater Archaeology Branch of the QAR Shipwreck Project in Morehead City, NC.

Appendix A: Bonnet's Letter to the Governor

Following is the actual letter Stede Bonnet wrote to the governor of South Carolina:

Honoured Sir,

I have presumed, on the Confidence of your eminent Goodness, to throw myself, after this manner, at your Feet, to implore you'll graciously by pleased to look upon me with tender Bowels of Pity and Compassion; and believe me to be the most miserable Man this Day breathing: That the Tears proceeding from my most sorrowful Soul may soften your Heart, and encline you to consider my dismal State, wholly, I must confess, unprepared to receive so soon the dreadful Execution you have been pleas'd to appoint me; and therefore beseech you to think me an Object of your Mercy.

For God Sake, good Sir, let the Oaths of three Christian Men weigh something with you, who are ready to depose, when you please to allow them the Liberty, the Compulsions I lay under in committing those Acts, for which I am doom'd to die.

I entreat you not to let me fall a Sacrifice to the Envy and ungodly Rage of some few Men, who, not being yet satisfied with Blood, feign to believe, that if I had the Happiness of a longer life in this World, I should still employ it in a wicked Manner; which, to remove that and all other Doubts with your Honour, I heartily beseech you'll permit me to live, and I'll voluntarily put it ever out of my Power, by separating all my Limbs from my Body, only reserving the Use of my Tongue, to call continually on, and pray to the Lord, my God, and mourn all my Days in Sackcloth and Ashes to work out confident Hopes of my Salvation, at the great and dreadful Day, when all righteous Souls shall receive their just Rewards: And to render your Honour a further Assurance of being incapable to prejudice any of my Fellow-Christians, if I was so wickedly bent; I humbly beg you will (as Punishment of my Sins for my poor Soul's Sake) indent me a menial Servant to your Honour and this Government, during my Life, and send me up to the farthest Inland Garrison or Settlement in the Country, or any otherways you'll be pleased to dispose of me; and likewise that you'll receive the Willingness of my Friends to be bound for my good Behaviour, and constant Attendance to your Commands.

I once more beg for the Lord's Sake, dear Sir, that as you are a Christian, you will be so charitable to have Mercy and Compassion on my miserable Soul, but too newly awaked from a Habit of Sin, to entertain so confident Hopes and Assurance of its being received into the Arms of my blessed Jesus, as is necessary to reconcile me to so speedy a Death; wherefore, as my Life, Blood, Reputation of my Family, and future happy State lyes entirely at your Disposal; I implore you to consider me with a Christian and charitable Heart, and determine mercifully of me, that may ever acknowledge and esteem you next to God my Saviour; and oblige me ever to pray, that our heavenly Father will also forgive your Trespasses.

Now the God of Peace, that brought again from the Dead our Lord Jesus, that great Shepherd of the Sheep, thro' the Blood of the everlasting Covenant, make you perfect in every good Work to do his Will, working in you that which is well pleasing in his Sight, thro' Jesus Christ, to who be Glory for ever and ever, is the hearty Prayer of

Your Honour's Most miserable,
and Afflicted Servant,
STEDE BONNET

Appendix B: Convicted Pirates

Following is an alphabetical list of the pirates tried, found guilty, and receiving the sentence of death in Charles-Town, South Carolina, in the fall of 1718:

- ☐ Alexander Annand, from Jamaica
- ☐ Job Bayley, from London
- ☐ Stede Bonnet, from Barbados
- ☐ Jonathan Booth, (possibly Samuel Booth) from Charles-Town
- ☐ Robert Boyd, from Bath, North Carolina
- ☐ John Brierly, alias Timberhead, from Bath, North Carolina
- ☐ Thomas Carman, from Maidstone in Kent
- ☐ George Dunkin, from Glascow
- ☐ William Eddy, alias Neddy, from Aberdeen
- ☐ William Hewet, from Jamaica
- ☐ Matthew King, from Jamaica
- ☐ William Livers, alias Elvis (maybe Evis)
- ☐ John Levit, from North Carolina
- ☐ Zachariah Long, from Holland
- ☐ John Lopez, from Oporto
- ☐ William Morrison, from Jamaica
- ☐ James Mullet, alias Millet, from London
- ☐ Neal Paterson, from Aberdeen
- ☐ Daniel Perry, from Guernsey
- ☐ Thomas Price, from Bristol
- ☐ John Dutch, (possibly John Ridge) from London
- ☐ James Robbins, alias Rattle, from London
- ☐ Edward Robinson, from New-Castle upon Tine
- ☐ George Rose, from Glascow
- ☐ William Scot, from Aberdeen
- ☐ John-William Smith, from Charles-Town
- ☐ John Thomas, from Jamaica
- ☐ Robert Tucker, from Jamaica
- ☐ Henry Virgin, from Bristol
- ☐ James Wilson, from Dublin

Appendix C: Men Charged and Acquitted

The following men were acquitted of all charges:

- ☐ Jonathan Clark
- ☐ Thomas Gerrard
- ☐ Thomas Nichols
- ☐ Rowland Sharpe

Primary Resources:

1. Butler, Lindley S. Pirates, *Privateers, and Rebel Raiders of the Carolina Coast*. Chapel Hill: The University of North Carolina Press, 2000.

2. Cordingly, David. *Under the Black Flag: The Romance and Reality of Life Among the Pirates*. New York: Random House Publishing Group, 2006.

3. Defoe, Daniel. *The General History of the Pyrates*. Edited by Manuel Schonhorn. Mineola, NY: Dover Publications, 1999.

4. Journeys to the Bottom of the Sea – Blackbeard's Revenge. Dir. Danielle Peck. Produced by BBC Science. 2006.

5. Rankin, Hugh F. *The Pirates of Colonial North Carolina*. Raleigh: State Department of Archives and History, 2001.

6. *The Tryals of Major Stede Bonnet and Other Pirates, viz...Who were all condemn'd for Piracy...At the Admiralty Sessions held at Charles-Town in the Province of South Carolina, on Tuesday the 28th of October, 1718. and by several Adjournments continued to Wednesday the 12th of November, following. To which is Prefix'd An Account of the Taking of the said Major Bonnet, and the rest of the Pirates*. London: Benjamin Cowse, 1719.

Secondary Resources:

7. Appell, Jonathan. "RE: early 1700's cemeteries." E-mail to Leeann Cronk. 5 July, 2006.

8. Arts and Entertainment Network, Digital Ranch, History Channel, A & E Home Video, and New Video Group. True Caribbean Pirates. [New York, N.Y.]: A&E Home Video, 2006.

9. Berry, Joyce. "What was it Really Like in the Olden Days?" Hygiene and Cosmetics Through the Ages. 10 December, 2006. <http://www.fortklock.com/cosmeticshygiene.htm>

10. Bjorndal, Karen A. "Re: Sea turtle question." E-mail to Leeann Cronk. 6 June, 2006. (Karen Bjorndal is the director of the Archie Carr Center for Sea Turtle Research at the University of Florida.)

11. Bourne, Joel K. "Blackbeard Lives." National Geographic July 2006: 146-161.

12. Bordsen, John. "Prowling with Pirates." The Charlotte Observer 12 August, 2001.

13. "Bristol – 1700 Onwards." Bristol. June 30, 2006. <http://www.brisray.com/bristol/bhist6.htm>

14. Callahan, John "Jack". Personal Interview. April, 2007. Dr. Callahan is a geologist who has worked extensively and directly with the "Queen Anne's Revenge Project".

15. "Church History Page." First Presbyterian Church in Jamaica. June 17, 2006. <http://www.firstchurchjamaica.org/church history.htm>

16. Clunies, Sandra MacLean and Bruce Roberts. Pirates of the Southern Coast. Norfolk, Virginia: Letton Gooch Printers, 2002.

17. "The Comparative Value of Money between Britain and the Colonies." June 30, 2006. <http://www.coins.nd.edu/ColCurrency/CurrencyIntros/IntroValue.html>

18. Cordingly, David (Consulting Editor). *Pirates, Terror on the High Seas from the Caribbean to the South China Sea.* North Dighton, MA: JG Press, 1998.

19. Dalrymple, Alexander. *An Historical Collection of the Several Voyages and Discoveries in the South Pacific Ocean.* London: Printed by the Author, 1770.

20. Douglass, William. *A Summary, Historical and Political, of the First Planting, Progressive Improvements, and Present State of the British Settlements in North America.* Boston: Reprinted for R. Baldwin, 1755.

21. "Eighteenth-Century Currencies and Exchange Rates." hudsonrivervalley.net. July 1, 2006.
<http://www.hudsonrivervalley.net/AMERICANBOOK/18.html>

22. History Channel, and Arts and Entertainment Network. Modern Marvels: Pirate Tech, 2006.

23. Hyneman, Jamie and Adam Savage. MythBusters: Pirate Tech. Silver Spring, MD: Discovery Communications, 2007.

24. Jack, Albert. *Red Herrings & White Elephants – The Origins of the Phrases We Use Ever Day.* New York: HarperCollins, 2004.

25. Johnson, Capt. Charles. *The History of the Lives and Actions of the Most Famous Highwaymen, Street-Robbers, &c. &c. &c. to which is Added a Genuine Account of the Voyages and Plunders of the Most Noted Pirates.* Edinburgh: John Thomas Jun and Co., 1814.

26. Konstam, Angus. *Blackbeard: America's Most Notorious Pirate.* New Jersey: John Wiley & Sons, Inc., 2006.

27. Marine Research Society. *The Pirate's Own Book: Authentic Narratives of the Most Celebrated Sea Robbers.* 1837. Reprinted in 1993.

28. Moore, David. "A General History of Blackbeard the Pirate, the Queen Anne's Revenge and the Adventure." The Queen Anne's Revenge Project. North Carolina Maritime Museum, North Carolina Division of Archives and History. May 30, 2006.
<http://www.ah.dcr.state.nc.us/qar/rcorner/genhistory.htm>

29. Park, Edwards. "To Bathe or Not to Bathe: Coming Clean in Colonial America." The Colonial Williamsburg Foundation. 2006. <http://www.colonialwilliamsburg.com/foundation/journal/Autumn00/bathe.cfm>

30. Poyer, Reverend John. "Baptisms Grace Church, Jamaica." Page 268. New York 1710-1731. Transcribed by Peter Devine, February 2004. June 17th, 2006. <http://olivetreegenealogy.com/nn/church/jamaicanybpt.shtml>

31. Purcell, William. "Chasing the Rogue Pirate Blackbeard – Professor's Discoveries May Lead to Scientific Treasure." Appalachian Today Spring 2001: 5-7.

32. Purefoy, James. Blackbeard, terror at sea. [Washington, D.C.]: National Geographic, 2006.

33. Roberts, Nancy. "Re: Blackbeard/Bonnet/Israel Morton." E-mail to Leeann Cronk. 28 July, 2006.

34. Roberts, Nancy. "Re: Israel Morton." E-mail to Leeann Cronk. 30 July, 2006.

35. Rowlett, Russ. "English Customary Weights and Measures." How Many? A Dictionary of Units of Measurement. University of North Carolina at Chapel Hill. 10 August, 2006. <http://www.unc.edu/~rowlett/units/custom.html>

36. Selinger, Gail. "Re: Pirate Fiction Plot Summary." Email to Leeann Cronk. 2 January, 2007.

37. Selinger, Gail. "Re: Stede Bonnet Question." Email to Leeann Cronk. 9 December, 2006.

38. Selinger, Gail. "Re: Writing Questions Reply." Email to Leeann Cronk. 18 December, 2006.

39. Selinger, Gail, with W. Thomas Smith Jr. The Complete Idiot's Guide to Pirates. New York: Penguin Group, 2006.

40. Seymour, John. The Forgotten Arts & Crafts. London: Dorling Kindersley, 2001.

41. "Small Change Coinage of ca. 1700 and Related Coinage Proposals: Introduction."
<http://www.coins.nd.edu/ColCurrency/CurrencyIntros/IntroValue.html>

42. Sobel, Debbie. "Re: sea turtle question." E-mail to Leeann Cronk. 6 June, 2006.

43. Wiggins, Trip. "How Much Do I Owe You? – Money in Colonial Virginia." The Rappahannock Gazette – Newsletter of the Rappahannock Colonial Heritage Society, Inc. 5:2 Fall 2002 1, 4-7.

44. Wilde-Ramsing, Mark. "Re: QAR Documents." E-mail to Leeann Cronk. 4 October, 2006. Mark Wilde-Ramsing is the Director of the Queen Anne's Revenge Project.

45. Wilde-Ramsing, Mark. "Re: QAR Bell." E-mail to Leeann Cronk. 9 August, 2006.

46. Wilkinson, S. The Voyages and Adventures of Edward Teach. Boston: Book Printing Office, 1808.

47. Williamson, Hugh. The History of North Carolina. Philadelphia: Thomas Dobson at the Stone House (Fry and Kammerer, Printers), 1812.

48. Wolfinger, Kirk, John Chatterton, Melanie Paul, and Michael Richard Plowman. Deepsea Detectives: Blackbeard's Mystery Ship. A & E Television Networks, 2005.

Thank you for reading *The Pirate's Revenge*. Please consider leaving a review on Amazon, Goodreads, or other venues, and be sure to tell others about it!

~ ~ ~

L.N. Cronk is the best-selling author of the highly-rated, contemporary Christian fiction *Chop, Chop* series. The first book in the series—the award-winning *Chop, Chop*—is a complete, stand-alone novel which is available **free** for most eReaders including Kindle, Nook, and iPad.

Heather Frey Blanton is the best-selling author of the top-rated historical fiction novel, *A Lady in Defiance*. Heather has also worked as a journalist for newspapers, magazines, and blogs and has spent decades in the corporate communications field, as well, writing about everything from software to motorcycles.

Barbie Halaby, founder of Monocle Editing, provides editing and proofreading services to scholarly journals, publishers, authors, and other businesses. She offers fine-tuning or intensive line editing to bring an author's work to the next level. Clients include Routledge, the University of Toronto Press, and Palgrave Macmillan, as well as self-published authors and those seeking traditional publishing routes.

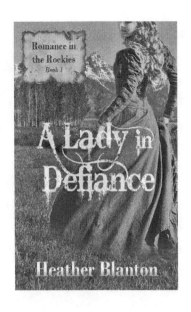

Heather Blanton's best-selling, top-rated

A Lady in Defiance

Romance in the Rockies Book 1

. . . IT'S HIS TOWN AND HE DARES GOD TO STEP FOOT IN IT.

Charles McIntyre owns everything and everyone in the lawless, godless mining town of Defiance. When three good, Christian sisters from his beloved South show up stranded, alone, and offering to open a "nice" hotel, he is intrigued enough to let them stay—especially since he sees feisty middle sister Naomi as a possible conquest.

But Naomi, angry with God for widowing her, wants no part of Defiance or the saloon-owning, prostitute-keeping Mr. McIntyre. It would seem however, that God has gone to elaborate lengths to bring them together. The question is, "Why?" Does God really have a plan for each and every life?

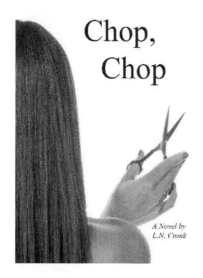

Chop,
Chop

*A Novel by
L.N. Cronk*

L.N. Cronk's
best-selling,
award-winning,
top-rated

Chop, Chop

CONTEMPORARY CHRISTIAN FICTION

Ever since Laci was a little girl she's been growing out her pretty, brown hair and chopping it off to send to Locks of Love. When Greg moves into town and finds out what she's doing, he thinks it's a great idea . . . so he starts doing it too! It's just one of the things that reserved, young David must tolerate as their friendship grows throughout the years. As they near adulthood, they grow not only closer to each other, but closer to God as well. David finds himself content in every way, but when tragedy occurs David must struggle to find his way back to God.

Chop, Chop is an award-winning, coming-of-age novel dealing with everyday experiences that anyone can relate to, but culminating in one catastrophic event that no one would ever want to. A story of friendship, loss, and forgiveness, *Chop, Chop* is a complete, stand-alone novel that is available in paperback, or as a **free** eBook, for most eReaders including Kindle, Nook and iPad.

F
CRO

8/26/14

31367281R00133

WW
LB
LH

Made in the USA
Charleston, SC
15 July 2014